I0705942

STICKING AROUND

BOSTON BUCKS

CATHRYN FOX

COPYRIGHT

Sticking Around
Copyright 2024 by Cathryn Fox
Published by Cathryn Fox

ALL RIGHTS RESERVED. Without limiting the rights under copyright reserved above, no part of this publication may be reproduced, stored in or introduced into a retrieval system, or transmitted, in any form, or by any means (electronic, mechanical, photocopying, recording, or otherwise) without the prior written permission of both the copyright owner and the above publisher of this book.

This is a work of fiction. Names, characters, places, brands, media, and incidents are either the product of the author's imagination or are used fictitiously. The author acknowledges the trademarked status and trademark owners of various products referenced in this work of fiction, which have been used without permission. The publication/use of these trademarks is not authorized, associated with, or sponsored by the trademark owners.

This e-book is licensed for your personal enjoyment only. This e-book may not be re-sold or given away to other people. If you would like to share this book with another person, please purchase an additional copy for each recipient. If you're reading this book and did not purchase it, or it was not purchased for your use only, then please return to your favorite e-book retailer and purchase your own copy. Thank you for respecting the hard work of this author.

ISBN Ebook: 978-1-998943-62-3

ISBN Print: 978-1-998943-61-6

1

BRADY

"Who the fuck is making all that noise?"

I mute the TV, but don't wait for a response to that question. That would be a little ludicrous, even for a jokester like me, considering I'm all alone inside this luxurious suite my buddy Noah offered up to me last month. Yeah, I couldn't spend one more night in the same house as Theo Wagner. Sure, Theo is great on the ice, but a total asshole in real life and I'm pretty sure—unlike him—I've outgrown the bunnies and the parties. Not that I'd let anyone know that. Being the loudest and most outgoing is what's expected of me, but dammit, I'm so fucking tired of it.

The noise sounds again. Are drawers slamming? I push off the sofa and walk to the window. It's late, and Noah, his wife Brighton and their daughter Camryn are at their summer house just outside the city of Boston. No way would they be coming home this late at night. Besides, their car isn't in the driveway. The only vehicle out there is mine, which means it's conceivable that someone is breaking into their wing of the house, which is just across the hall from me.

I walk to my door and pull it open. Light seeps out from the door across the hall and I listen for sounds. I take a few steps and look over the handcrafted guardrail that showcases a grand entranceway downstairs. The house is old and huge, located in Sparrow Springs, and nestled in behind White Beach Resort. Creaking sounds aren't uncommon, but this was more of a bang. The downstairs door is shut tight, and as far as I know, outside of Noah and his family, I'm the only one with a key.

I walk to the other door, put my hand on the doorknob and listen for a moment. This time, my ears are met with silence and I consider going back to my place to rewatch last season's final game, and possibly beat myself up a little more for not stopping Pittsburgh's winning goal. A thrilling Saturday night, I know.

I'm about to turn, but think better of it. I should probably check to make sure no one is stealing from my buddy. He didn't hesitate to offer up the empty wing inside his house, and keeping the place protected is the least I can do in exchange for his kindness. It's not like I can't afford my own house. I just don't want the commitment.

I turn the knob and push the door open, glancing around the empty living room. A lamp on the side table glows yellow. Did Noah leave that on when he left yesterday? Maybe, and maybe I didn't notice the glow.

"Hello," I call out, and go still. This time, I do wait for an answer. When none comes, I carefully walk farther into the room. I stop to check the den, guest bathroom, kitchen, and the latch on the door leading out to the wide wrap-around patio. Locked. A good sign. After finding half the place untouched, I relax my shoulders and shake out my fists. I head back to the living room and that's when I notice light coming from one of the rooms down the long hall.

Shit.

I glance around and the first thing I see is a fireplace poker. I snatch it up and slowly make my way down the hall. A bang reverberates off the walls in one of the rooms. I don't know which one. I've been in Noah's place numerous times. I've just never ventured into their sleeping space.

Walking quietly, until I come to the lit room, I hold the poker out, ready to call out to the burglar invading my buddy's place. But the door swings open and I come face to face—or rather, face to naked body—with none other than Melanie Clark, the bartender at the White Beach resort. She hates me.

"What the..."

She gasps, covers her body with her hands—not that she's doing a great job of hiding all her sweet curves—and jumps back when her gaze lands on the poker.

"I'm sorry," I say quickly and hold my hand up palm out. "I thought someone was breaking in." I shake my head. "I nearly hit you with the poker."

Her gaze drops. "You were going to poke me with that thing?"

I shift my stance, her nakedness doing the craziest things to me. Wait, is she referring to the steel rod in my hand...or in my pants? Shit. "Sorry...there was a bang, and a poke. I mean, there wasn't a poke. I grabbed a poker." I run agitated hands through my hair. "Dammit, I could have poked you."

Jesus, dude, stop saying bang and poke.

"I'm glad you didn't."

Yeah, okay, I get it. She hates me and I'm sure there is underlying meaning to her words.

"Do you always walk around naked?" I ask.

She backs up some more, and when she does, I spot a big fluffy towel on the hook. I jerk my hand out and she jumps back. "What are you doing?"

I tug the towel from the hook and avert my gaze as I hold it out to her. "Getting you a towel. What did you think I was doing?"

"I..." She takes the towel from me.

Saving her the trouble of explaining, I say, "I wasn't going to touch you."

From her reaction, clearly that would have been awful for her. But I don't touch women who don't want to be touched—or any woman who despises me.

A rustling sound fills the silence of the room as she covers her body. "I'm decent."

I turn back to her and try not to let my gaze drop to the knot on the towel, or admire the way it squeezes her breasts together.

"To answer your question, no, I don't always walk around naked. I forgot my pajamas in the bedroom, and it's hot in here. I thought I was alone, so I was just going to cross the hall and get them."

"Sorry about all this." I back up and angle my body, so she can get to her room. "I didn't know you were here."

She takes a step and hesitates. "Brighton didn't text you to let you know I'd be staying here for the weekend?"

I scratch my head. "No."

She nods. "It was pretty last minute, and it probably just slipped her mind. She's been busy getting the baby's room ready, here and at their summer home."

"Right." It was just last week that Brighton announced to us all that she was pregnant. We'd all been at their summer home for a barbecue when she shared the news. It was also at that barbecue when Melanie shot me down after I asked her out. That was pretty embarrassing. When I said I was going to talk to her, my buddies Conner and Gunther warned me that she wouldn't have anything to do with a guy like me and I stupidly put a bet on it—and lost.

Melanie isn't the kind of woman who is into quick hook-ups, and that's all I can give her. Hell, she's a couple of years older than me and is working on her Master's of Psychology. Right there...that's another reason not to get close. I don't need her in my brain, discovering and dissecting the shit I keep bottled up. No fucking way.

Emotions are weakness, Brady. You're the man of the house now so grow a set.

As my mother's warm, encouraging words ping around inside my brain, Melanie walks past me, the freshly showered scent of her skin teasing my senses.

"I should go."

"Okay," she calls out from her room.

Poker still in hand, I take one step down the hall and hesitate. "Is everything okay?"

The sound of a zipper peeling open fills the hall. "Yeah, why?"

"I just mean, it's late and you're staying here for the night." My muscles tense again, every worst possible scenario playing out in my brain. I haven't seen her with any men, but if she's here late at night maybe... "Are you hurt?" Silence. I suck in a breath and wait for her to answer. She remains silent so I take a step toward her room, and find her dressed in pajama shorts, her back to the door. "Melanie, if someone hurt you..."

She pulls a T-shirt from a duffle bag full of clothes on the bed and slips into it. Angling her head, her gaze meets mine and for the first time since I've known her, she directs a smile my way. I nearly drop to my knees. Jesus Christ, she is so fucking beautiful. So different from the flighty bunnies who swarm us before and after games. Maturity looks good on this woman.

I'd look good on this woman.

Better yet, she'd look good on me.

I swallow hard at those thoughts because that's never going to happen.

"What are you going to do, Brady?" She plants one hand on her hip, and juts it out, a challenging gleam in her eyes. "Go fight him?"

"Damn right. No one hurts those I care about."

She arches a brow. "You're saying you care about me?"

"You're good friends with my friends, so yeah, by proxy, I care about you." I shrug, and pretend her dislike of me doesn't hurt. "Even though you don't like me."

Her eyes soften. "I never said that, Brady."

I snort out a laugh. "Not in words, no."

"I just...don't date."

She's leaving off...guys like you. That's okay. I get it. I do have a reputation, and she's a serious woman, a bartender here at the resort, working toward a better life. I totally respect that, and I know the work that goes into achieving a successful career.

"No one hurt you?" I ask.

"No. My roommate recently got engaged, and her guy is over a lot. I like him. He's not giving me trouble, but our thin walls sure as heck are." She grins, and I laugh at that.

"Gotcha, and I'm here because of my roommate. While our walls aren't thin, there's just a lot of partying going on. Got me drove."

She angles her head, her gaze moving over my face, a careful assessment, and I try not to squirm. I'm not much into being evaluated—off the ice. Her brow lifts. "Is the player played out?"

I open my mouth, wanting to tell the truth, but instead say, "Not in this lifetime, babe."

And this is why you could never get with a woman like Melanie, you ass.

But emotions are for pussies right, Mom? Jesus I've been taught to keep them buried for so long, it'd take the jaws of life to break them open.

"I should go." Before she says anything else, I head down the hall, put the poker back and make a beeline for the door.

"Brady," she calls out and I come to an abrupt halt. "Got me drove?"

I chuckle. "It means, something is annoying me. Newfound-land saying."

"It's kind of funny."

"Yes, b'y."

She smiles at me again, and breath leaves my lungs in a whoosh. "Do they call you Coddy, because your last name is Fisher, and you're a Newfoundlander and Newfoundland is known for its cod fishing?"

"No."

"No?" One brow arches up, clearly surprised by my one-word answer. "Care to explain then?"

Since she seems rather amused by my Newfie language, I say, "I'll put da ol' slut on. Put da wood in da 'ole an we'll 'ave a yarn."

"Ol' slut? You better not be talking about me." I laugh and she folds her arms, waiting for an explanation.

"It means, I'll put the kettle on." I point to the open door and continue to translate. "Close the door and we'll have a chat."

"Then you'll tell me how you got the nickname Coddy."

"Yes, b'y!" I give her a mischievous grin, full of promise. "It's a Newfoundland thing, and if you're up to it, I can screech you in and you can become an honorary Newfoundlander."

A mixture of curiosity and suspicion moves into her big blue eyes. "Screech me in?" A grin flirts with the corner of her mouth, and dammit, it's all I can do not to drag her to me and cover her lips with mine. "Do I dare ask?"

2

MELANIE

I shake my head hard and fast at Brady as he stands near the door and explains his Newfoundland language and traditions to me. Oddly enough there are two goalies on the team with the same first name, but it's easy to tell the difference by their accents, and to be honest the other Brady is a bigger player off the ice and that's saying something.

I hold my hands up and back away. Honestly, I knew better than to ask. "No way. Uh uh. Not in this lifetime. I shouldn't have asked." I make a mental note not to ask Brady anything ever again.

"Oh, come on, it's not that bad." He jerks his thumb over his shoulder. "I can be right back with a cod and some screech. Won't take but a minute."

"Brady, no. I am not kissing a cod, or any fish, or drinking screech? What exactly is screech, anyway?"

"It's rum and you have the order wrong. You drink and then kiss the cod."

I scrunch up my nose. "It'd have to be the biggest glass of rum ever to get me to do that."

"That can be arranged."

"Forget it. I am not kissing anything of yours." A shiver goes through me and I'm not one hundred percent sure it's from the thoughts of kissing a fish. Maybe it has more to do with how sexual that sounds, and I'm not all convinced that I'd never kiss anything of his.

Get it together, Melanie.

"You Newfoundlanders are crazy people."

He folds his arms across a broad chest and it's all I can do not to admire his big biceps. "Don't knock it until you try it."

"I'm not kissing a slimy fish."

"It's not slimy. It might be shiny, but it's dry, and hey, fun fact, they can taste like cucumber when really fresh. Dad used to be a fisherman, and sometimes when I helped, we cooked them right off the boats."

Is that how he got all those muscles? "Eating a fish and kissing one is different."

He pulls his phone out, and his fingers fly across the screen. "True, and did you know cod are high in protein and low in fat?"

"You know an awful lot about cod."

"That's why they call me Coddy." He holds his phone out to me. "Look, once you're screeched in, we can print off this official certificate and you can be an honorary Newfoundlander."

"I think I'm going to stick with being a Bostonian."

"Suit yourself. But if you ever come to Newfoundland with me, it's happening." He laughs and the sound curls around me. I take in his handsome features as his phone pings and he checks the message. Honestly, I don't hate Brady, but I can see why he thinks I do. I've just not really given him the time of day before. I haven't been rude to him, but I shut down his advances as fast as they come—which clearly means, I'm never going to Newfoundland with him.

He's cute enough, though. Actually, he's drop dead gorgeous, and that's half the problem. The man is a joker, the life of a party kind of guy, one who has women throwing their panties at him, even in the streets. At least that's what Brighton—owner of this gorgeous house I'm in, and the resort beside it, where I bartend—told me.

I'm finally getting my life together and I don't need some younger guy, a player on and off the ice, messing around inside my head. I'm the psychologist here. I'm the one who's supposed to be doing the messing and the helping. Nothing about getting involved with Brady is going to help me.

Okay, maybe that's not entirely true. Getting involved with him sure would help soothe the needy ache between my legs. One that makes its presence known every time he's in the room—and yes, even times when he's not. Dammit.

He shakes his head and tucks his phone away. I note his grin and ask, "Everything okay?"

"Yeah, that was Noah, letting me know you'd be staying here this weekend." He laughs. "I told him I nearly poked you."

"What?" I practically shriek. "Did you explain what you meant?" Oh, good God, I can only imagine what's going through Noah's mind and naturally he's going to say something to Brighton.

"Nah, let him think on that for a while."

"Brady!" This time I do shriek. I don't want Noah—yeah, we're friends, but he's also my boss—to think I'm messing around with his teammate in his house, when he's been kind enough to offer me a place to stay for the weekend. Just then, my phone pings.

I throw one hand out and my voice is dripping with sarcasm when I say, "Geez, I wonder who that is." Brady gives me a smirk, and like I said…joker. I hurry across the room, snatch my phone off the coffee table and read the message from Brighton.

"Brady poked you? Do tell."

I can't help but laugh and I look up to see that irresistible look on Brady's face, but unlike one of his bunnies, I'm immune to it.

Or not.

You are not hooking up with him, girl.

I growl at him. "You're a troublemaker, Brady Fisher."

He playfully shrugs it off. "I've been called worse."

Is the man ever serious? All the more reason for me not to get involved, right? Or maybe all the right reasons for me *to* get involved. Because maybe there is something I'd like to ask Brady…or rather, ask for.

I nearly choke on that last thought.

What did you just say about not hooking up?

The truth is, the last thing I'm looking for is a serious relationship, or any kind of relationship. I have zero interest in losing any kind of focus, and when it comes to asking for anything, not going to happen. There's always a hitch and a promise—or should I say, a broken promise.

Even though Brighton and I grew close over the last year, asking for a place to spend the weekend was so incredibly hard for me. No one gives without expecting something in return—that's how life works—so I'll pay them back, somehow. Not financially, because it's all I can do to pay my upcoming tuition by the end of October, but maybe I'll take Camryn out for the day and give them some much needed adult time before the pre-season kicks in.

I stare at my phone and more messages come in from Brighton. "What am I supposed to tell her? Nothing is going to come out right over text."

"Call her, straighten it out. How about I run out and grab us an order of fish and chips? All that talk about cod has made me hungry."

My stomach takes that moment to grumble. I should say no, and send him back to his wing in this big house, but I worked a long shift tonight and was going to have toast before bed. Fish and chips do sound yummy.

"Just make sure the cod is cooked," I warn, trying for my most stern look, or at least one that says I'm only in this for the food, but from his grin, I guess I failed. I wave toward the door. "Go, I need to call Brighton and straighten this out, thanks to you."

"At least I didn't say anything about banging."

I pick the pillow up off the sofa and toss it at him. He laughs, catches it, and sets it down before heading out the door, and despite everything I said about not hooking up with this man, I stare at his ass until the door closes.

With a heavy sigh, I phone Brighton and her voice is full of surprise and mischief when she answers with, "I want all the details."

"There are no details," I blurt out. "Nothing happened and nothing ever will happen."

She makes a sad noise, like she's upset by that. "Then what did he mean?"

"He didn't know I was here and he heard a bang—"

"Bang?"

"Ohmigod, Brighton, really? You're as bad as Brady."

"If I remember correctly, you were the one who told me to be bad where Noah was concerned. I sure am glad I took your advice." I exhale a happy sigh and I have no doubt she's rubbing her growing tummy as she stares lovingly at the man of her dreams.

I lift my chin a little higher, even though she can't see me. "That's because I give good advice." I've been working my butt off on my masters, getting the highest grades in my class, and I'm quite proud of my accomplishment.

"That's right," she tells me. "Your problem is, you can dish advice, but you can't take it."

"First, I didn't know I had a problem, and second, I thought your degree was in business management and tourism, not psychology."

"Truth, now tell me about this poke and bang."

"It's the other way around," I begin, remembering how I had the kiss and screech order mixed up. "I had just showered after getting in and Brady didn't think anyone was here, and I was banging around, and when I came out of the bathroom, he had a fireplace poker in his hand. So, bang and poke. All innocent." As I let her mull on that, curiosity gets the better of me, I ask, "Anyway, what is this advice you think I should take?"

"That maybe a bang and a poke is just what the doctor ordered."

"And now you're a doctor," I shoot out, exasperated, as my mind goes down a path I shouldn't let it.

"You have been working too hard lately, Mel." She goes serious when she adds, "You need some *you* time. Or rather *you* and *Brady* time. He's totally into you, and don't think I haven't noticed the way you've been eyeing him."

I square my shoulders in defense. "I have not been eyeing anyone."

It's a lie. I have been staring so hard I'm pretty sure my eyeballs are doing that bulging cartoon thing. I mean, the man in his jersey is one thing, but a bathing suit at the rooftop pool, showcasing a hard lean body that makes me want to rip my panties from my hips...

A small chuckle from the other end of the phone pulls me back. "Are you still there?"

I plop down onto the sofa, happy the summer will soon be coming to an end, and the men on the Boston Bucks team won't be having rooftop pool parties that heat me up more than the hot summer sun.

"You know who he is and what he's like."

I nod and toy with a loose thread on the hem of my pajama T-shirt. I never thought about how unflattering this old thing must look on me. Not that I thought I'd be entertaining the opposite sex tonight and it's been a long damn time since I bought anything remotely sexy for bed.

Don't think about sex.

"True."

I hear Noah in the background, and realize I'm probably keeping them from bed.

Don't think about bed.

"You know he's not looking for anything serious," she continues.

"Again, true."

"Then why not rip into that man's boxers and have a bang and a poke?"

I am going to kill Brady for joking around with Noah like that, but hey, I was the one who brought up bang. Ugh. "I'm dressed in an old pair of pajama shorts and a T-shirt and they're both frayed. That does not scream seduce me."

"Seduce him then, and I'm sure he doesn't care what you're wearing. Better yet, be naked when he gets back." I open my mouth to protest and I'm sure she senses a rant coming, but I close it again when she adds, "Hey, I have some sexy, new lingerie in my second from the top drawer. I never got a chance to use it before getting pregnant. The tags are still on them. They're all yours. Besides it would look better on you than me. You have the right curves."

Heat gathers between my legs, and I think it's my neglected sex telling me to listen to my friend. "I am not—"

"Brady is young and enjoying life. He might be just what you need right now." Before I can protest, she adds, "I bet he knows all kinds of ways to have fun and take your mind off school, work, and finding a new place to live."

"I'm not kissing a damn cod," I mumble, as I think about other things that I can kiss.

"What?" she asks laughing.

"Nothing." A whine I have no control over what squeaks out of my throat because everything Brighton is saying sounds just about awesome right now. "You're killing me, Brighton." I glance up and check the time. Honestly, I should be digging out my books, not thinking about a hot Newfie coming back with fish and chips and then jumping his body. Key word there, *should* be...

"Listen, I really appreciate you letting me stay here this weekend. I just couldn't take one more night of my roomie and her man." Maybe part of the reason is all their sex sounds were driving me crazy was because I wanted a little of what they had. "I'm going to start searching for my own place first thing tomorrow. They're banging like bunnies."

There's that word again.

"You know you can stay for as long as you like. The downstairs of the house has bedrooms we're not using, and a full kitchen and living room. This is more of a house than we need."

The downstairs is huge, she's right about that. It's equipped with a kitchen, living room and plenty of sleeping quarters. When you walk in the estate's front door, there's a grand staircase leading to a landing with two fully equipped wings on either side. The downstairs used to be used for staff, but

Noah had reassigned them all when he bought the resort. He wanted his privacy.

"Thanks, I appreciate that, but I don't want to put anyone out."

She snickers. "I know someone who wants to be put out."

"Are you still on that?" I shake my head. What is happening in my life and when did Brighton decide to play matchmaker?

"If you play your cards right, you could be on that, too."

BRADY

As I consider Melanie's predicament and the reason she too is staying at our friends' place, I can't help but chuckle. Here I thought we didn't have anything in common, and it turns out we do. We both have noisy roommates and we both love cod—when it's cooked.

The delicious smells of the food in the brown paper bag in the back seat make my stomach grumble as I pull up in front of my buddy's giant estate and kill the ignition. I shake my head and grin as I look up at the living room window. Who would have thought I'd be sharing a late-night meal with a woman who always shoots me down, but says she doesn't hate me. I get it, though. She's working hard to get her master's degree and why would she want to get messed up with a guy like me? Nothing good can come from that.

That thought brings a pang to my stomach, and as it curls into a tight, near-debilitating knot, I swallow against the bile punching into my throat. Working to settle my stomach, I jump from the front seat and grab the bag of food from the back seat. I hit the fob, and when I'm able to get control of that unwanted rush of emotions, I start toward the front door.

I make it only one step when my phone pings and I stop to pull it from my pocket, somehow hoping it's Melanie, but knowing that's impossible. We haven't exchanged numbers. Although, maybe Brighton gave her mine when she called. Then another thought hits. What if she's messaging to say she's changed her mind?

Why does the idea of that bug me so much? I can have my pick of any girl I want, and I'm not trying to sound like an asshole here. It's just that lately all that partying, with girls who only want me for a good time, has lost its appeal.

I check my phone to see that it's my mother, and my heart thumps. I won't take her call now. She'll be half asleep from her meds, and it's hard to understand her when she's slurring, especially when she swallows them down with alcohol. Besides, I already made a big deposit into her account earlier today. She'll find it in the morning when she's clear headed. Although, I'm not so sure she's ever clear headed anymore.

I tuck my phone away and start toward the house again, only to come to a resounding halt when I'm suddenly hit with an epiphany. Melanie thinks I'm a player—a fucking joker. Why wouldn't she? After my father died and I'd become 'the man of the house' I was told to stop acting like a whiny eight-year-old. I never thought I was whiny, or overly emotional. Christ, I was close to my dad and his death nearly destroyed me. But no tears were allowed to be shed in my mother's household.

Maybe if Melanie knew who I really was, things would be different. If I was myself with her, maybe she'd like that guy. My chest deflates. Or maybe she wouldn't. But what the hell do I have to lose? Honestly, I've been hiding my emotions for so long, I'm not even sure I know how to be real in the face of others.

I use my key and let myself into the massive estate, and I glance up the big staircase and take a couple of deep breaths before I dart up the stairs. I force one foot in front of the other, and find the door to Melanie's side of the house cracked open. Didn't I close that when I left? Now I really am worried about an intruder. I push it open and hope to find a serious Melanie on the sofa studying—or simply waiting for me—but the room is empty. A measure of panic hits.

Maybe she just went to bed.

I head to the kitchen and drop the food on the counter, then tiptoe down the hall to find the most gorgeous woman I've ever set eyes on laid out on the bed in the spare room. Jesus. She's no longer dressed in her frayed shorts and T-shirt, which I happened to find real, and sexy and perfect on her. Now she's dressed in some sexy number, and while I like it—damn, who am I kidding, I kind of love it—it's not what drew me to her in the first place.

"Hey." I swallow. What the hell is going on? She can't be dressed like this for me, right? She sits up, and smooths her hand over her stomach, and I take in the way the lacy lingerie hugs her breasts. Because I'm a damn idiot and completely off my game, I ask, "Were you expecting company? I thought we were eating?"

"I'm hungry, Brady." I nod and I'm about to let her know that I came back with food like we discussed, but she crooks her finger. "But not for food."

Sweet mother of God and all that is holy.

What the fuck is happening right now? I hesitate for the briefest of seconds and something moves over her face, something that looks a lot like worry—that I might not find her desirable. Christ, I always took her for a self-assured, confident woman, but hey, maybe that's just what she puts out there. I, for one, personally know we're not always who we appear to be.

She makes a move to get up, and I reach over my head, grip my T-shirt and tear it off. A little gasp catches in her throat, and while my cock is reacting, there's a part of me that sort of hoped she might have seen me as something other than a boy toy, but that's ridiculous. It's all I ever put out there, all I ever allow people to see. Why should she be any different? And why did I think for one second anyone ever wanted anyone but the guy who could give them a bucking good time, a long running joke describing the men on the Bucks team.

"This what you want?" I ask, the air around us charging, growing hot and volatile, and as blood leaves my brain, I no longer wonder about her sudden change of heart. Hell, maybe she had a discussion with Brighton. I know my buddy Noah hasn't been discouraging my attraction to his friend. In fact, he told me when I wasn't looking, Melanie was.

"Get over here, Coddy."

I grin and take a deliberate, measured step toward her. Working to forget my darker thoughts and give her the playful man she's looking for, I jokingly say, "I'm coming, *Lanie*."

She cocks her brows. "No one has ever shortened my name quite like that before."

"Yeah, that's a first?" I like having firsts with her.

She pushes the blankets down and my cock thickens even more when I see long silky legs that lead up to black lace panties that light a fire to my already wild imagination.

"Yes, and I have to say, I like it." I pop the button on my jeans and close the distance between us. My dick jumps and pokes out of the top of my boxers.

"Something else you like, Lanie?" I tease.

"I'll have to see more before I can decide, Coddy."

I grin and tug my pants down, exposing myself to her. Her lips part, a pink flush flashing across her cheeks as I take my dick into my hand, rubbing it from base to crown as it thickens even more. "How about now?" I ask and her gaze lifts, locks with mine.

"Yes..."

"I already know I like what I see." I let my gaze travel from the tips of her toes, up her silky legs, over her flat stomach to her gorgeous full breasts. "But that doesn't mean I don't want to see more."

Her chest rises and falls rapidly, and while it's easy to tell she's excited and wants this, I sense a bit of apprehension. What changed in her since I was gone? I'm not sure, but now is probably not the time to ask. Now is the time to give her what she wants. I press my knee into the bed and climb on, staying up on both knees as I slowly inch toward her, and position myself between her legs, after inching them open.

I want to ask if she's okay, if it's been a while, but she doesn't want any kind of serious conversation from me right now, so instead I run my hands up her legs, and gauge her reaction as I come close to her barely covered pussy. "You need this?" I ask instead. She nods, and I slide a finger between her thighs.

"Why don't you open up these gorgeous legs and show me much how much you want my cock."

Her eyes go wide, and I sense that no one has ever talked to her quite like that before. But I also sense that she likes it. She slowly inches her legs open and I wet my lips, dying for a taste of her as I turn all my focus to pleasing her.

I touch the lace material on her panties and slowly tug on the band, exposing only the top of her sex. I take in her pretty pink clit, swollen and needy, begging to be touched. I zero in on it, and bend forward, letting my warm breath fall over her beautiful nub when I say, "I really like what I see."

"Brady..." I slide my tongue over her clit, and she moans as her hips lift. "God, Brady."

I kiss her and tug her panties down a bit more, exposing more of her lush body. Her hands slide through my hair and she holds me to her, and I bite back a chuckle. Yeah, I'm pretty sure it's been a while for her.

I inch back, and she whimpers at the loss of my mouth as I slide her panties down and toss them away. But that whimper turns to a moan as I flatten myself on the bed, slide my hands under her backside, and lift her sex to my hungry mouth.

She gasps. "Oh yes. Just like that."

I kiss her gorgeous pussy deeply, loving the flavor of her on my tongue. Jesus, I don't think I've ever tasted anything so sweet or addictive. Yeah, I'm going to want more of this. My cock thickens, and I need to get these fucking pants down before I rupture my throbbing cock. I just don't want to take my mouth off of her to do it.

I slide my tongue over her, and her juices wet my mouth as I eat at her like a man starved. She moves her hips, and her sexy little moans of pleasure reverberate through my body. I lift my head to see her, taking in the heat in her eyes as she watches. I slide a thick finger inside her and her mouth opens. "I never knew how hungry I was until this moment."

"No?" God, I love how breathless she sounds.

"No, and I'm going to eat and eat until I've had my fill." She nods, clearly liking that idea. I bury my face between her legs again, a man on a mission to quench his thirst, and his appetite. I explore her with my finger, wanting to discover all her likes. I slide it in and out as I circle her clit with my tongue, and when her moans grow louder, I crook my finger to press the rough pad of my finger against the hot bundle of nerves inside. Her body tightens around me and I take a deep breath to center myself as my cock throbs, wanting in on the action.

I fuck her with my finger and slide another in for a snug fit, and she trembles around me as she quietly chants my name. I pull out and slide back in and glance up to see her rolling her head from side to side, her hair a tangled mess beneath her. I fucking love watching her come undone beneath my ministrations.

Lost in pleasure, she moans something incomprehensible, and with the soft blade of my tongue, I apply more pressure, taking her to the edge of ecstasy. She tugs at my hair, giving in to the pleasure pulling at her, and as she lets go, her hot cum spills from her body and coats my fingers and mouth. I lap at her, drinking in every last drop, but it's going to take more than one night with her to quench my thirst, and that sort of frightens me.

I lightly pet her, and blow a breath over her quivering clit, and her entire body quakes. I stay between her legs, wanting to fall asleep with my mouth on her, my fingers inside, but my cock has other ideas. So does Lanie, judging by the way she's tugging at me. I lift my head and grin at her.

"Something else you need to see?" I ask, and swipe my tongue over my lips to taste her again.

She crooks her finger, and I'm about to climb up her body when she stops me. "Up on your knees."

I momentarily hesitate. If it wasn't for the lust in her eyes, I'd think she was tossing me out after her orgasm. I do as she says, and my cock twitches, my crown spurting pre-cum as it peeks out of my boxers. I arch a questioning brow as she gives me a mischievous grin.

"I think I might want to kiss the cod," she says, a hint of laughter in her eyes.

My head rears back. "What? Seriously? Right now?"

She chuckles, tugs on my pants until my cock springs free, and wraps her small fingers around the length of me. I run a shaky hand through my hair. "Jesus."

Her warm breath washes over my crown and pre-cum drips from my slit as she leans in and wraps her full lips around my cock. "Mmm..." she murmurs around a mouthful.

"Fuck me."

She tilts her head, and lust, need and playfulness dance in her eyes as they meet mine. My cock slips from her mouth and she murmurs. "That sounds like a good idea. But I'm not quite done kissing the cod." Her hot breath fires my blood and she turns her attention to my cock as it throbs in her hand. She stares at me, like she's committing my dick to memory. I'm about to tell her she doesn't have to sketch anything with her mind. Fuck, she can put her mouth on me anytime she likes. My words fall off as she stretches her lips around me again, taking me to the back of her throat.

I grip her long dark hair and wrap it around my hands as she takes me deep, and since it's actually been a while for me too, I bite down on my cheek to tamp down the urgency in my body. Her hands follow the action of her wet mouth, and I shake, pleasure gripping hard, too hard. I need to be inside her. Need to feel her hot body wrapped around my dick.

I gently tug on her hair. "Fuck. Now."

My dick stands at attention as she takes her mouth off my cock, and I give a little push until she's flat on her back, her legs wide open, her body mine for the taking. I jump from the bed, my eyes still on her sexy body, her nipples specifically as they poke through the lace material, and tear my pants and boxers from my body in record time. So much for tamping down my urgency.

She writhes and lifts her hips, welcoming me into her body and seconds before I climb over her, I remember I need a condom. I might not be having a lot of sex lately, but I'm always prepared. I pick my pants back up and her eyes drop, the lust in her eyes clearing as she turns her head and stares off into the distance. What, did the sight of the foil package momentarily bring her back to reality and remind her that I'm simply a fuck toy? But that's all she wants, right? Hell, it's what I want, too.

Don't forget that you can't be anything more to her, dude.

At that painful reminder, I rip into the foil and lust returns to her eyes as I sheathe myself and climb back onto the bed. I fall over her and tug down on her lacy top to expose her perfect pink nipples. Hard and pert and waiting for my mouth. I admire her for a moment the same way she admired my cock and wet my lips before murmuring, "So pretty."

Her arms snake around my body, and her fingers explore my back as I lick on a bud and pull it into my mouth to savor the sweet taste and texture. So fucking good. She arches into my mouth as I move my body, settling my dick between her legs. I rock against her, rubbing up against her wet heat.

"Brady, please," she whimpers, and I tear my mouth from her breast and press them to her mouth for a ferocious kiss as I shift until my cock is at her opening. Our eyes meet and lock and I soften the kiss, our lips barely touching as I move my hips and slide all the way inside her. Our groans mingle, and despite the need hitting like a runaway puck, I go still, basking in the way her muscles tighten around my dick. I slide my arms under her, holding her tight as I sink into her body, wanting to curl up in it and live there forever. But she has other plans. She begins to move, bucking against me, and I go up on my elbows so I can piston into her.

I pull out and slide back in, and a garbled noise catches in my throat as I briefly close my eyes as intense pleasure builds inside me. "Jesus, you are so hot and tight."

"More. Harder."

I grip the back of her shoulders, and give her what she wants, despite the fact that I'm so fucking close to the edge. I pound into her body, hammer her with my cock, my brain completely shutting down, nothing mattering but this woman and the pleasure I want to give her.

"Brady, God...Brady."

"I know," I breathe out, and capture her mouth with mine again, swallowing her cries of pleasure so they can live inside me. We move together, each giving and taking until her sweet pussy tightens around my cock, and the second her hot juices sear me, I throw my head back and let go, pumping seed into the condom, and oddly enough, wishing we didn't have the barrier.

I stay inside her as I flop down on top of her body, shifting so I don't crush her with my weight. She runs her fingers lightly over my back, and it tickles but I like it. After a long moment she breaks the quiet.

"I really needed that." I lift my head and she smiles at me. "Thank you."

I laugh. "I don't think anyone has ever thanked me for sex before."

Surprise lights her face. "Really, never? I mean, you've been with..."

Her words fall off and that familiar troubled look is back.

"No, never, and I should be the one thanking you," I say, working to keep things light.

"Now that's a first for me, too."

I don't ask her how many men she's been with, but I'm so curious about her. She said she doesn't date, but has she ever been in a serious relationship? If so, how long ago and is that the reason she doesn't date anymore? But those are questions for people trying to get to know each other and that's not really what's happening here. I might have thought about letting her see the real me earlier, but that would have been a mistake. I must have been concussing our something. When it comes right down to it, I can't offer her anything. I can't commit. Jesus, I have enough responsibility on my shoulders as it is; it's weighing on me so heavily, it's a surprise I can breathe sometimes.

Yeah, I just can't take on anymore, because fuck, what if she needed me and I couldn't be there? What if I failed her, like I failed others? My mind goes back to the accident I had at sixteen, and I push it back fast. Now is not the time to let painful thoughts rise to the surface. Now is the time to flee from the bed like I always do.

Okay, so why the hell aren't I moving?

● 4

MELANIE

I stare at Brady's broad back and admire the way his muscles ripple as he throws his legs over the side of the bed and stands. He glances at his clothes on the floor and I fully expect him to pull them on and go back to his wing of the house. After all, that's his move. Yeah, Brady Fisher doesn't stick around after sex, and it shouldn't be any different with me. In fact, I don't want it to be.

I open my mouth about to say something, anything, but he speaks first. "Be right back." My heart jumps into my throat as he walks to the door and steps into the hall, still naked. What the heck is he doing? Across the hall, I hear water running in the sink and I grab the blankets to pull them up, wanting to get into the bathroom myself to wash up.

He comes back into the room, a warm, satisfied look on his face, as he gives me his famous bad boy grin. "Why are you covered up? I've already seen everything, Lanie, and I've been inside you." Heat rushes to my face. "Can you please take the blankets off?"

I swallow. "Since you're asking so nicely."

Unsure of what's going on here, I slowly slide the blankets off, feeling a little exposed and vulnerable beneath his intense gaze, but I also feel admired and maybe cherished, not that I would really know what it's like to feel those things. The truth is, I've always wanted to feel special, but I know that comes with a price and broken promises.

"Spread your legs," he commands in a soft voice, and that's when I see the washcloth in his hands. No freaking way. My heart pounds against my chest as I slowly inch my legs open. Brady sits on the bed, and the second he puts the warm cloth on my sex to wash me up, my throat tightens with emotions I really don't want to feel. What is going on here? This isn't the Brady I know, and while I liked that Brady—accepting him for who he is, because hey, we all have flaws—I like this man before me, too.

"Doing okay?" he asks, probably because I've gone as still as a stealth soldier. Dark, questioning eyes meet mine and I give a tight nod.

"You?"

"I'm doing great, Lanie." He moves on the bed, and bends to give me a soft, easy kiss. The kind of kiss familiar lovers give one another and it messes with my brain and body.

Before I can think better of it, I blurt out, "Kiss me like that again, and I'll never let you out of this bed."

He chuckles. "While I'm up for that, I'm not quite up for that." He gestures with a nod to his soft cock, and I laugh with him. "Besides, we have fish and chips in the kitchen and I want to feed you." His lids fall, veiling his eyes as he removes the cloth from between my legs, and there's a different kind of seriousness about him when he adds, "You worked all night, and then exerted yourself with me, and I want you to have your strength tomorrow for studying." At the mention of food, my stomach grumbles. He puts his hand on my belly. "See. Come on. Let's get dressed and I'll heat the food up."

He stands and tugs on his jeans and T-shirt, and I climb back into my frayed pajama shorts and T-shirt. I lift my arms and let them fall to my sides. "All ready."

"Yeah," he murmurs and gazes at me, his eyes holding the same amount of desire as they did when he found me in the lingerie. Maybe a little more, which is kind of strange.

He puts his hand on the small of my back and it sends warm shivers through my body as he guides me to the door. We go down the hall and into the kitchen and the delicious scent of French fries reaches my nostrils.

"Mmm, grease and carbs before bed."

"I start hard training and restrictive dieting soon, so I'm going to eat everything I want..." His gaze drops to my body. "...all I want, before that."

I gulp at the heat in his eyes and something in the way he says, 'eat everything I want' makes me think he's talking about me. We can't fall into bed together ever again, though. That first time was a little intense—maybe because it's been so long for me, or maybe not—but nevertheless, I can't let myself feel anything for Brady. Love, lust and even like comes with conditions, and I will not ever put myself out there again. No one, and I mean no one in this world is going to dupe me...not again.

He turns the oven on and starts opening cupboards. "It's best to heat this in the oven. The microwave will make it soggy, and that's just nasty."

"Smart." I grab a sheet pan for him, and he goes to work on opening the boxes. I line the pan with parchment paper and he carefully places the fish and chips on it with big hands—hands that I crave to feel on my body again. Once he has the fish pieces and fries arranged the way he wants, he slides the pan into the oven. Funny, he's delicate about it, and it seems so contrary to his personality, and the way he plays hockey.

"Did you spend a lot of time in a kitchen?" I ask.

"Yeah."

I wait for him to elaborate, but he doesn't. "Thirsty?" I ask, and open the fridge. Catching me by surprise, he steps up behind me, slides his arms around my body and pulls me against his chest. I gasp as he puts his mouth near my ear, his breath hot on the outer shell.

"I was, but you helped me quench it."

I gulp at his dirty words, yet I like them a lot. I don't tell him that. I don't need to. The quiver that raced through my body, and no doubt reverberated through his, told him everything he needs to know. Jeez, I think I might be an easy read for him.

"But I'll have a glass of pop."

I chuckle at that. "Here we call it soda."

"Well, now that you're officially a Newfoundlander, you can call it pop."

I turn to him and put my arms around his shoulders. I lift my gaze, because he's damn tall, and remind him. "I'm not officially a Newfoundlander. I didn't kiss a real cod."

He winks. "Close enough."

"Nope, that's cheating and lying, and if there is one thing I hate in this world, it's liars." I lean into him, my lips close to his, even though I just told myself we couldn't ever fall into bed together, but hey this is the kitchen so that's different. Talk about logical thinking at its worst.

He curls his hand through my hair and gently tugs until my lips part. "Look, do you want to kiss a real cod or do you want to take the break I'm giving you."

"Did you not hear the part about me hating liars?"

"Fair enough. We'll do the ceremony then."

"Who says I even want to be an honorary Newfoundlander, anyway?"

"Who wouldn't want to be?" He shoots out, feigning exasperation. "We're the best kind of people, duckie."

I nod. "If you say so. I'll have to take your word on it since you're the only Newfoundlander I know." He arches a brow, waiting for me to add more. I brush my lips over his and whisper, "And for the record, you were the best."

His grin is wide and playful as he picks me up, sets me on the counter, wraps his big hand around the back of my neck and presses his lips to mine for a mind-numbing kiss full of heat and promise. I widen my legs and he grips my hips, pulling me closer to the edge, and his more than ready cock presses hard against my sex.

Dammit, you can't do this again, girl.

Just when I'm about to beg him to pick me up and take me back to the bed, my brain registers a beeping sound. I slowly inch back and take in the lust in Brady's confused eyes, and note the way his chest is rising and falling as he takes deep, labored breaths. I blink, working to clear my own lust and that's when I clue in. The fridge door is beeping because we left it open.

"Fridge," I manage to get out as the lust in his eyes turns to laughter.

"Oh, is that what that was? I couldn't figure it out." He inches back and I instantly miss the warmth between my legs. He swallows. "I'm thirsty again and since you need to eat and I refuse to take you back to bed to quench it, until you do, I'll need to drink a *pop*."

He emphasizes the word pop and I chuckle. "Grab me a soda, please."

He lifts a brow, looking less than impressed as he turns to grab two bottles from the fridge. I stare at his perfect back-side, unapologetically admiring his body as he cracks the plastic cap on mine before handing it over. I take a long pull from the bottle, and he does the same.

He sets his bottle on the counter and checks the food. "Just about ready. Want to grab the plates and ketchup?" I do as he asks, and also grab some napkins and utensils.

I glance into the other room. "Want to eat in the living room and flick on something?"

"More than anything," he answers.

"I'll bring these things in." I leave the plates and carry our drinks and everything else into the living room. I set them down beside my books and remember that I was supposed to be studying tonight before my upcoming big exam. I guess I can cram tomorrow before work, and I don't have to make the commute back to my place because I'm staying here for the weekend. I find it so hard to study on the bus.

But staying here another night means Brady will be just a stone's throw away...again. Is that good or bad? I'm going to go with the latter. I pick up the remote and find some mindless sitcom that we can watch as we eat. I'm about to head back to the kitchen, when Brady appears with two plates full of delicious food.

"Dinner is served."

He sets the plates on the coffee table and drops down into the sofa, patting the seat beside him. "Right here, Lanie."

I grin, loving the nickname he gave me. "You got it, Coddy."

I sit, put my plate on my lap and squirt ketchup all over my food. "Do you want some fish and chips with your ketchup?" he asks, but then goes ahead and covers his with even more ketchup. "You know, in Newfoundland we mostly dip our fries into mayo."

I crinkle up my nose. "That's kind of disgusting."

"It's actually pretty good."

"Do you want me to get you some mayo?" I ask.

He shakes his head. "No, because then I'd want you to try it and I need to ease you into being a Newfoundlander. We're a lot to take at once."

I swallow at that. Yeah, I did take a lot of him at once and he had a lot to give. I toss a fry into my mouth and stare at the television, not really focused on the sitcom. My mind is too busy, my body keyed up, even though I should be lethargic after sex—and I know why I'm not. Okay, time to address the elephant in the room, and no, I'm not talking about the trunk he's working with between his legs.

"Brady?"

I lift my head and when I catch the way his eyes are narrowing in on me, my stomach tightens. Damn, he's been waiting for this conversation. I take a breath and stare at some distant point behind his shoulder as I work to form a coherent thought, and not cause tension between us. Heck, we see a lot of each other now that he's living here and I don't want to walk around avoiding him.

"What's on your mind, Lanie?"

My gaze drops to my plate and even though my appetite is dwindling, I dip a French fry into the ketchup, but I don't eat it. I just play with it. "I'm sorry you thought I hated you. I guess I can understand why. But I don't hate you. I think you're a nice guy."

"Good to know. I'd hate for you to sleep with a guy you didn't like." I angle my head, my gaze moving over the shadows on his face. When my eyes meet his, there's something very serious about him. "But I get the feeling there's something else you're trying to tell me."

I chuckle quietly and pretend to throw the fry at him. "Hey, I'm the psychologist. Stop reading into things and stay out of my head."

"Oh, so you're the only one allowed to read into things because you're doing your master's degree in psychology?" I grin at him and play coy, like I haven't been reading into what we've been doing all night. "Wait, have you been trying to get into my head?" he asks.

"No." I shrug. "You're a pretty easy read, Brady."

He nods as I eye him. Wait, what the hell just flashed in his eyes before he blinked it away? Was it hurt? Am I missing something here? God, if I am, I worry about my career choice. I'm trained to see beneath the layers.

Before I can examine that hurt deeper, Brady turns things back to me. "I'm not wrong though, am I?"

"Right, you're not wrong. What we did was fun. There's no denying that." I crinkle my nose up and even though I know he's a guy with a revolving door, and almost never sleeps with the same woman twice, for some reason I feel like I need to be gentle with him. "We just probably shouldn't do it again." I glance at my stack of books on the coffee table. "I have school and work, and I've been bussing back and forth from my apartment for a month now because my car broke down and I need to find another place to live. Plus...I mean, you have a lot of girls waiting their turn." Shoot, why did I add that? Was it to remind him, or me? Honestly, I don't know. I think those orgasms are messing with my brain. I am not looking for anything from this man.

He nods and shrugs it off like it's nothing. "Yeah, sure. I totally understand." A smile stretches his lips but doesn't reach his eyes. "Hey, you know me." He kicks his legs out, looking relaxed, but there's a tightness in his shoulders. Maybe it wouldn't be visible to most, but I see the tenseness. "I'm here for a bucking good time, and nothing more."

My chest tightens, a trickle of unease skating down my spine as I examine that quick flash of pain that disappears as quickly as it appeared. Have I been reading this man all wrong? Is there more to him?

He winks at me, his deep laugh curling around me as he says, "As far as I know, I'm the only Newfoundlander around here, so if you ever get 'hungry' again, and want to kiss a cod..." He pokes his thumb into his chest. "I'm your guy." His deep laugh curls around me. "Something you need to see, just knock on my door. I keep boxes of condoms at my place."

Okay, I guess not, and I'm not sure how I feel about that.

He bites into his fish and goes quiet. Once done, he glances at me. "Did you grow up wanting to be a psychologist?"

"Did you grow up wanting to be a hockey player?"

His shoulders tighten. "Right."

Shoot, that wasn't nice. I just don't like talking about my past, because it was pretty damn shitty. "I'm sorry, Brady."

"Nothing to be sorry for."

"I didn't grow up wanting to be a psychologist. I wanted to be a painter, actually."

He smiles. "Really." I nod. "Why the change of heart?"

He goes completely serious, like he really wants to hear my story. As his hand lightly touches mine, the small sweep of his thumb over my wrist is tender, comforting, like a warm familiar sweater keeping me warm and perhaps it's that that has me blurting out, "I want to help others—especially children—and be there for them because there was no one there for me."

5

BRADY

My heart jumps into my throat and for a quick minute I can't even fill my lungs. My thoughts race back to my childhood, to the small town I grew up in, and how my life changed drastically after my father died. I became the man of the house, immediately charged with taking care of my mother, who was debilitated with...well, she never did get a proper diagnosis. Or if she did, it was not my business. I was there for her always, and I still am. What must it have been like for Melanie to have no one to rely on?

I set my fork down and it clinks against my plate. "I'm sorry."

Eyes wide, horror crosses her face, and she gives a fast shake of her head as she sets her fork down too. "I'm sorry," she begins, shaking her head hard as she clasps her hands together. "I'm not looking for sympathy." Her voice is rushed, hurried as she continues with, "I don't even know why I told you that."

My heart drops to my stomach, pushing the fish I'd just eaten back up into my throat. "Right. I understand." What I understand is that I'm a guy she only wants to have a good time with. Not a guy she could ever open her heart to. Honestly, it seems to be the curse of our team. I'm not the only one known for a good time.

The stricken look on her face at having said too much is a reminder of what I am to her and what's going on here. Hell, I could easily tell her I'm not that guy. But then what? What if she wanted more? Shit, she just told me she was basically neglected and never had anyone who was there for her. Christ, I can't be there for her. I'm not the guy to take that on. I have far too many people counting on me. Every time I hand over money, I'm reminded of that and the fact that Dad's life insurance paid for my hockey instead of buying things my mother needed. It's always there, lingering in every conversation I have with my mother.

I'm also reminded of that one time, right after I got my license at sixteen and decided to have some fun, for once in my life. I ended up in the hospital and couldn't be there for anyone...and then my mother...she had a fall. Bile punches into my throat and a hard quiver goes through me at that horrible reminder, and the painful aftermath. That's when I realized I need to be on high alert at all times. I don't ever want to let anyone down again. Not my mother, my family, my team...or this woman. Jesus, I never should have slept with Lanie. I like her too much to let her down, and I just can't be responsible for even one more person.

"Brady?"

I pull myself out of my stupor and focus on the beautiful woman beside me. She just told me something private and personal, and even though she's regretting it, that doesn't mean I didn't hear it or that she doesn't need some kind of response. "If you want to talk about it…"

She gives a wave of her hand to brush it off, but she just put painful parts of her past out there and it's hard for me to unhear them—not that I'd want to, but it does give me a bit of insight into her, and will always remind me I'm not the guy she needs in her life. "No, what I'm trying to say is you don't need to hear my problems."

I shift on the sofa until I'm facing her, and cup the side of her face. Despite the lecture I'd just given myself, and knowing better than to get in deeper, I ask, "Do you want to open your own practice, or do you want to work in a school, or maybe a hospital?"

Her eyes soften, the former panic somewhat dissipating, but she's still a bit guarded. "I'd actually like to work in a school. I think a less clinical environment can help kids open up."

"What grades are you thinking?"

"All, really. It wasn't until my senior year that I managed to talk to someone. I guess I'd still been holding out hope until then."

She spent all those years holding out hope that someone would be there for her. Jesus. What the fuck was wrong with her parents?

I wait for her to continue, but instead she stifles a yawn. I give her a reassuring smile, understanding she's ready to call it a night, and maybe this conversation has gone as far as she wants to take it. "You're going to be great, Lanie."

"Did you always want to play hockey?" she asks quietly, her voice less harsh and accusatory this time, and I pull her to me, resting her head on my shoulder.

"Dad always wanted me to play hockey. He loved watching the games and I think he secretly wanted to be in the NHL. The opportunity was never there for him growing up, though." A beat of silence and then, "He died on the fishing boats when I was only eight. It was just Mom and me after that." Fuck, what is going on with the two of us? I lean forward to look out the window. Must be a full moon or something. I don't talk about my past and I'm pretty damn sure Melanie doesn't either. She wouldn't have acted like she just spilled military secrets if she had.

Her head lifts and concerned eyes meet mine. "I'm sorry, Brady."

"Thanks. It was a long time ago." I yawn, and lightly run my fingers through her hair. "I still miss him."

I guide her head back to my shoulders. "Of course, you do. Is your…"

"Yeah, Mom is alive. Still in Paradise, a small coastal town in Newfoundland. That's where I grew up."

"Paradise, sounds nice."

I snort at that and when she tries to lift her head, I gently hold it down, worried that my eyes hold too much pain. "Yeah, tourists seem to like the icebergs."

"Wow, I'd love to see one someday. Paradise…" she murmurs under her breath.

I laugh and without thinking, say, "Our sign says 'population four hundred'. I can't tell you how many times the kids would mess with the sign and spray paint, 'A nice place to visit, wouldn't want to live there.'"

"That's awful." She looks at me. "Wait, you did that, didn't you?"

I lift my chin an inch. "I admit to nothing."

"Is your family still there?"

"Lots of aunts, uncles, and cousins. All in the fishing industry. I'm the only one who ever left."

"You must miss them." I don't answer. I stay quiet and she continues, "Fishing. That's big business in Newfoundland, right?"

"Used to be. Lots of overfishing and new government regulations make it hard now."

"I had no idea."

"There is a processing plant in the next city over, though. Good steady work there. If you're fit and able," I add.

She eyes me, a careful assessment and I try not to shift, because yeah, I think I've said too much. I'm not sure why. There's no full moon out there. Could it be because I'm comfortable with her? If that's the case, I'd better watch myself. This can't go anywhere.

"It's so weird," she admits.

"What is?" I touch her cheek as she continues to study me, as if seeing me in a different light all of a sudden. "Do I have ketchup on my face or something?"

"No, it's just... I guess I just pictured you having a different upbringing. I mean you played for Scotia Academy, in Halifax, Nova Scotia, right?"

I nod. "How did you know that?"

"Brighton told me."

"Talking about me, were you?" I tease.

She rolls her eyes and makes a pfft, sound, but it does little to crush my ego, considering I don't have one. She'd probably be surprised to learn that. "Yeah, now that I think about it, I overheard it."

I grin. "Okay, let's get back to your point. I went to Scotia Academy, so what?"

"I don't know. I guess it was kind of wrong of me to make assumptions, but a private school for hockey, then the NHL."

"Ah, I get it. You think I was born with a silver spoon." She shrugs, but the answer is in her eyes. "I was born with silver all right, but it was a fishing lure, and you'd find it in a cod's mouth, not mine."

She chuckles at that and before she can ask any more questions, I stretch out my arms. "I should get you to bed and get back to my own. I refuse to be the reason you're too tired to study tomorrow."

She chuckles lightly. "If you were, I wouldn't be mad."

My cock instantly thickens at the warm neediness in her voice. Dammit, I'm suddenly needy too and I can't help but think we're both in need of touch because of those painful memories we revisited.

I shift to see her and she lifts her head. "Are you saying what I think you're saying?"

Her grin is warm and seductive. "If you think I'm saying the fish you bought was good, but I'd rather taste my 'Coddy,' then yes."

Leave, Brady.

One working brain cell kicks in. "Wait." I pinch the bridge of my nose before that braincell can find its way out. "You said, we probably shouldn't do this again."

She crinkles up her nose, and her hand lands on my thigh. Every muscle in my body reacts to her soft touch. "I did, didn't I?" She turns contemplative. "I said *probably*, and probably means in all likelihood, but I think there's a little wiggle room there, right?"

"Are you trying to say you're going to wiggle for me, Lanie?"

"Would you like that?"

"Fuck yeah."

She laughs and there's a new kind of warmth about her this evening. Perhaps it's because we're tired, everything about us less frenzied. "How about one more for the road, Coddy?"

Before I can answer—and obviously I'm going to agree, because hey, I'm a man, and I like this woman—she pushes to her feet, and gives an exaggerated swish of her hips as she saunters away. While nearly every bone in my body is encouraging me to run the other way, there is only one bone in charge at the moment, and it's honing its coordinates in on the sexy woman luring me back to her bed.

I stand, leaving our plates on the coffee table to clean later, flick off the TV and follow her down the hall. I find her standing beside the bed, her lingerie on the floor. Her shoulders are tight, like she's remembering the seductress in that bed earlier and thinking that's how I like my women. Goddammit, she's so fucking wrong.

"Hey."

She spins to face me, and my heart tightens at the uncertainty on her face as shaky fingers work to smooth out her hair. Fuck, she's the most desirable woman I've ever met, and never has to feel uncertain around me.

"You are so fucking sexy." Her gaze drops to the discarded lingerie again. "Look at me." Her head jerks up and I close the distance between us, sliding my hand around her hips and tugging her body to mine. Her pelvis presses against my cock and this time I wiggle to show her exactly what she does to me, especially when she's dressed in her frayed shorts and T-shirt. I love the realness about her, but I don't tell her that. She wants to live a fantasy with me—that's what I am to all girls—and I like her, so I plan to give it to her.

I find her mouth and my kisses are less hurried this time. Her moan is soft, and the warmth in her tone wraps around me, tugging tight. Jesus, I like this woman, and to think I nearly poked her earlier. Well, I kind of did poke her and plan to do it again.

I slide my hands under her shirt and she lifts her arms, making it easier for me to discard it. I drop to my knees and tug down her shorts, pressing soft kisses to her quivering flesh. Once I have her naked, I drink her in, and lift my gaze to hers, to find her staring intently, her eyes brimming with need.

I stand back up, strip off my clothes and take her hand in mine as I lead her to the bed. We both look at our linked hands, and something about it makes us chuckle.

"The last time I held a man's hand was..." She thinks for a second and adds, "...never."

"The last time I held a man's hand was never, too." I love this new warmth and tenderness about us...even though I should just be fucking her and bailing, like I normally do.

"The last time you held a girl's hand?" she asks.

"Two days ago." She swallows and smiles, but it doesn't reach her eyes. I cup her cheek, press my lips to hers and whisper, "It was Camryn's. I took her to the playground to give Noah and Brighton a few minutes alone."

"Fun."

"Oh, it was fun, until she wanted me to push her on the swing and then kicked me in the nuts." This time Lanie laughs out loud and the sound trickles through me, making me forget about the pressures weighing me down. "You think that's funny."

She pouts and climbs onto the bed, staying on her knees as I stand beside the mattress. She puts her hands between my legs and cups my nuts. "No, Coddy, but how about I kiss them all better?"

6

MELANIE

I wake to find the other side of the bed empty and while I feel a moment of regret and disappointment at the loss of Brady's warm yet hard body beside me, my brain lets me know it's for the best. Despite that, I roll over and check for his warmth. The sheets are cold, his body long gone from my bed. Inhaling deeply, I breathe in the scent he left on my pillow, pulling it deep into my lungs as warm memories from last night come back to tease me.

I chuckle and put my hand over my face. Did I really tell him I'd kiss his balls and make them better? Heck, I didn't just tell him, I went ahead and did it, and the grunts and noises he made filled me with some strange kind of happiness. I've had sex before—not recently, no—but I've had sex. Not mind-blowing sex like I had last night, and none of the guys I've been with had me wanting to beg for it. Not that I've been with a lot, but still.

Honestly, I told Brady it could only be a one-time thing, only for it to end up being three times. Yes, we went two rounds after I lured him back to my bed. I'm not sure what was going on with me. Maybe it had something to do with the warm, understanding look on his face when I revealed a painful memory about my past. Then he shared something personal with me, and after those intimate moments, there was a closeness between us, one I'd never felt with any one before, and one I know better than to examine too closely. Brady Fisher, Coddy, is a player.

But is he, Melanie?

Heck, even if he wasn't, do I really want to dive into trying to figure out why a guy would pretend to be something he's not? That's too messed up for me, and the truth is, I'm too busy with school and life to take on that challenge. I've come too far to let anything stand in the way of me completing my masters, and helping the children who need it.

I push from my bed, my muscles tight and sore in the most glorious ways, and pull on my frayed pajama shorts and T-shirt, shoving my phone into the small pocket. I grin as I recall the look on Brady's face when he first saw me in them. I walk to my window and pull the curtains back. On the sandy shore in the distance, I spot early morning joggers, and a few parents out with their young ones. It's late August and the resort is in full swing, which is why I'm run off my feet bartending at night. That's okay. I need the money, and the tips, which are best on Saturday nights. Tonight will be insane, and that means there'll be no time for studying between guests. It's a real balancing game between making money and studying.

I sigh and walk down the hall and into the kitchen. The dishes have been done and my insides soar when I find a pod and little note by the coffee machine. Dammit, I really wish that note didn't make me feel this happy.

. . .

Try this hazelnut vanilla coffee. My buddy at Scotia Academy got me hooked and I special-order them in from Canada.

Shocked and pleased—maybe a little too much—that he left me a note and his special blend of coffee, a burst of warmth and happiness rolls through me. Why the heck would he do this? A thank you for last night, maybe?

Chuckling at his antics, I pick up the pod and examine it. "Looks like you're pod worthy, *Lanie*." I laugh as I say the nickname Brady bestowed upon me. I kind of like his spin on my name, especially when he whispers it in my ear in bed. A fine shiver goes through me and I try to shake it off. It's time to move on from last night, so I put the pod into the machine and press the start button. It gurgles for a second and then delicious smells fill my nostrils as it brews. I turn around to lean against the counter as I wait, and even though this isn't my place, it suddenly feels lonely without Brady. Will we hang out again tonight?

No. No. No.

Go ahead, have some fun for a change, girlfriend.

I shake my head because that is not conducive to keeping my focus on school, and my head in the game.

But the sex was so good, sweetie.

Yeah, but I need to guard myself against his charm because I understand the cost of love.

Maybe it will be different with him.

No, it's never different.

You're just afraid to take a chance.

That's right.

Brighton was right. You give advice but never take it yourself.

As I mentally debate with myself, the machine beeps, indicating my coffee is done, and I add a splash of milk before taking a big drink. "So good," I murmur to myself just as my cell phone pings. I snatch it from my pocket. Brighton. I have no idea why I thought it might be Brady. I put my finger over the screen. Ugh. Do I tell her the truth? Of course, I have to, because the one thing in this world I hate is liars.

I smile to make sure my voice is cheerful. "Good morning."

"Good morning to you too, Mel." A pause and then, "So, how was last night?"

"That bed is so comfortable. I slept well." Not a lie. I did sleep well when I finally did fall asleep.

"Really, that's all I get?"

I chuckle, and walk up to the patio door. "I have no idea what you're talking about."

Camryn yells something to Brighton in the background and muffled sounds come through the phone. A second later, she asks, "Is Brady there?"

"Nope."

"Ah, darn. I was hoping you two would hook up." I groan, not able to hold it in anymore. The truth is, I'm bursting to talk about him. Seriously, I just want to hear his name on my lips and that's all kinds of crazy. "Ohmigod, you did, didn't you? Did you wear the lingerie? Was he awesome?"

"Yes, and yes and yes, and why did you think Brady and I

would be so good together?" Does she see something in Brady I don't? If so, that would make me a terrible psychologist.

"You were, weren't you?"

"I mean yes. The sex was amazing. I just don't understand why you were playing matchmaker."

Honestly, marriage has changed her for the better. She's far more relaxed and so damn happy and I'm happy for her. Maybe even a bit envious. But marriage and relationships aren't for me.

"Look you needed a break, and why not get with someone who doesn't want more. Sex for sex, no strings."

My stomach tightens with that. If there is one thing my childhood taught me, it's that there are always strings. Always. Everyone wants something in return—I'm the prime example of that.

"Yeah. No strings."

"I'm just saying I was once you, Mel. All work and no play. Look at me now. I couldn't be happier."

"I'm so happy with the way things turned out for you, Brighton. Just remember, it's not like Brady and I are going to end up married, though, and please let's just keep this between us. I don't need anyone speculating when it's just a fast fling."

"I won't, and I know it's not serious, but why not have some fun with a guy who has been asking you out forever."

"Right." A sudden burst of unease cramps my stomach. "Actually, why do you think he's been asking me out forever? He can have any girl he wants. Why me?"

"Why not you? You're gorgeous, mature, got your life together, and maybe he's tired of the bunnies." I'm about to ask if she has evidence of that, and stop. I don't need to go digging where I have no business digging. This is just a fling. "Where is he?" she asks.

"I don't know. I woke up and he was gone." I take a sip of coffee, and laugh.

"What's funny?"

"He left me one of his hazelnut vanilla pods. Apparently, he orders them in from Canada." She gives a low, slow whistle. "What?"

"Last night must have been spectacular."

"It was, but why do you say that."

"That coffee is a running joke. He won't share it with anyone." My heart beats a little too fast at that revelation. "He likes to jog in the morning, on the beach."

"That's nice," I murmur, like his whereabouts don't really matter to me. I hear Brighton chuckle and guess I'm not coming off as nonchalant as I'd hoped.

I quietly unlock the patio door and step out. Laughter and voices from those playing on the beach reach my ears and brings a smile to my face. I take a sip of coffee and breathe in the briny smell of the ocean.

"I heard that."

"Heard what?" I ask.

"The click of the lock. You're out on the patio, looking for him."

"I'm on the patio getting a breath of fresh air before I start studying and go looking for a place to live." That thought gives me pause. Why the heck is Brady staying here at the resort, anyway? Sure, his roommate is giving him grief, but he's an NHL superstar. Why doesn't he just buy a place of his own?

"You know we have—"

I cut her off. "I know and I really appreciate everything, Brighton. You're a life saver. I owe you."

She makes a *pfft* sound. "If anything, I owe you. You were the one who helped me get back with Noah and I'll always be grateful."

"You don't owe me," I practically whisper, her words once again reminding me there's always an exchange. People want things in return. "Brighton, why is Brady staying here?"

"Same as you. Roommate troubles."

"He did tell me that, but is he looking for a place of his own?"

"Not that I know of."

"Why is that?"

"I guess you'll have to ask him that." Just then, Camryn calls out to Brighton again. "Be right there, Jellybean. Listen, I have to go. We're going to pick out some baby furniture. We won't be back until after dinner tomorrow. The place is yours. Have fun with Brady."

"Thanks, Brighton. Enjoy your weekend."

We end the call and while the conversation reminded me of my childhood and how I would do anything for my parents' love—which never came—there's also a lightness inside me, too. Would it really hurt to have sex again with Brady? Heck, would he even want it? He banged me, and I'm sure I'm another notch on his belt, and he probably wants to move on to his next conquest.

Why don't you find out, girlfriend?

I actually do feel more relaxed than yesterday, all the endorphins lowered my stress level and improved my mood. When you really think about it, that could help with my studying, maybe even make me more productive.

There I go again, worst reasoning at its best.

As I scan the sandy shore, I note a familiar figure jogging close to the water's edge and I wilt against the rail, my body quivering as I admire his broad, perfect body from afar. He's so tall and strong and muscular, it makes it easy to pick him out in a crowd. I continue to drink my delicious coffee as I continue to stare and even though I don't jog, I suddenly want to be on the beach, suddenly want to feel the ocean mist on my face, and the sand between my toes. Maybe a good, hard run will help with my reasoning abilities, and clear my lust-rattled brain—because I'm very close to taking Brighton's advice and going for it again.

I quickly finish my coffee, rinse my mug and tug on some clothes. Once dressed, I head outside and make my way to the beach, but Brady is nowhere to be found and I can't help but think that's good. Perhaps it's a sign that the less I see of him the better and I should probably pack my bag and head back to my apartment tonight. But right now, I should get my next endorphin boost from exercise.

I start off slow, speed walking near the water where the sand is packed, and I lift my face to the sun as it beats down on my warm body. I dodge a family playing frisbee and ignore the pang in my stomach. Even if I did get married, I'd never want to bring a child into this crazy world. With that thought banging around inside my brain, I work to shut down my maternal instincts at the sight before me.

I'm about to pick up the pace, when I catch movement out of my peripheral vision, and turn to spot Brady coming out of the surf, a ballcap pulled low on his head. My heart nearly stalls at the gorgeous sight and my body temperature goes from simmer to boil in a matter of seconds—and it has nothing to do with the hot morning sun.

A mischievous grin tugs at the corners of Brady's lips when he spots me and comes running toward me. Water droplets drip down his chest in delicious ways that mess with my brain and body.

"Brady," I warn, as he scoops me up and pulls me against his chest. His heartbeat is strong against my body, and mine pounds quickly in response.

"You're looking a little hot, Lanie." He starts toward the water again, a threat in his eyes, and I yelp and wrap my arms around him.

"Don't you dare."

"Dare?" He slows his steps when he reaches the surf. "Are we playing truth or dare?"

I shriek as cold water splashes up. "If we are, I pick truth."

He comes to a complete stop. "Okay then, truth it is." His body tightens, and he glances at some distant spot like he's waging a very serious war with himself—but that seriousness dies an abrupt death when he asks, "Want to bang again?"

7

BRADY

I know it's stupid. Asking this incredible, intelligent, mature woman such a question, when I should be running the other way, but dammit, I like her. Again, all the more reason to put a measure of distance between us. *What the fuck are you doing, bud?*

Water splashes against our bodies as I stand still in the surf, the gorgeous woman I slept with last night pressed against my body. A bevy of emotions move over her face, and I remind myself that she told me we couldn't have sex again—before we had sex again. Goddammit, she's as conflicted about all this as I am—she clearly has her own reasons for keeping her distance. I'm about to tell her to forget it, that I was just kidding—something anyone would believe when it comes to me—when she opens her mouth and I stop speaking, because fuck, I really want to hear the answer.

"Yes," she says quietly and air leaves my lungs in a fast whoosh, because despite everything, that's the answer I wanted to hear on her lips. She swallows and it's tight and labored. "But..."

"But what?" I manage to get out.

"Just sex. No commitment."

I instantly call on the Brady people know. "Hey, those are the rules I live by, babe," I shoot back, a stupid grin on my face, one I've perfected over the years.

She watches me carefully for a second and I almost turn my head, but that might make her wonder.

"And…" she continues. "Just until your pre-season starts." I nod, because I'll need my head in the game, and I can't let anything interfere with hockey. Christ, I have too many people counting on my paycheck, and I failed my team last year when we didn't win the cup. That nearly fucking killed me. "My fall semester starts in September, and it's my hardest courses," she adds. "If you can live with those terms, then—"

"Deal."

She turns coy, and grins. "My turn."

Since most of the blood has left my brain and this is no time to get a boner, I call on what little focus I have and try to figure out what she's talking about. "Your turn?"

She pokes my chest. *Poke and bang*. "Truth or dare?"

I laugh, and while I'd normally pick dare, since I don't want anyone knowing the truth about me, something compels me to act out of character. That makes me ask myself a question —do I want her to know the truth? Sure, I had a moment of weakness last night, and weakness means I need to grow a set. "Truth, unless of course you're going to dare me to take you to bed right now, and bang you."

She chuckles and then puckers her lips like she's in thought. "Actually, I'm going to hold off on asking a question."

"Oh, really." She slips a little in my arms, and I adjust her, her eyes widening when she feels my dick thickening against her hip. "What are you up to, Lanie?"

"Nothing, I just can't think of anything right now."

I doubt that, but if she wants to wait, then so be it. "I can think of something."

"Oh?"

"Yeah, taking you to bed right now." I slowly lower her, but continue to hold her against me when her feet hit the ground.

She moves against my semi-boner, and a hard quiver goes through her. Her cheeks turn a pretty shade of pink as vibrations skitter through me and settle in my cock. "While that is tempting..." She crinkles up her nose. "I do have to study. You kept me too busy last night."

I take her hand in mind and her gaze drops, studying our entwined fingers as I give a tug, setting us both into motion. "You said you wouldn't be mad."

"I'm not." Her head lifts as we walk the beach and she grins at me. Fuck, I love how it lights up her eyes.

"Good, I wouldn't want to stand in the way of your studying."

"You weren't standing," she says and we both laugh. Honestly, this woman is all work and no play. I've known her for a year, watched her work at the rooftop bar and study when things were quiet. There's a deep seriousness about her, but when she says things like that, I realize beneath it all, she's fun loving, but tries to keep that part of herself contained.

"How long did you set aside to study?" She frowns, checks the time on my phone, and that's when I realize what I said, and how it's coming across to her. "Hold it. I'm not rushing you.

Take all the time you need to study. That's not what I'm getting at."

She nods, the worry leaving her face. "I was going to put in a solid three hours."

"Do you take breaks?"

"Definitely, and I was going to use that time to search for a place to live."

I consider that for a moment. I don't have much to do today, other than rest up for conditioning on Monday. "Okay, I have a plan."

One brow raises. "You do? I told you—"

I sidestep a nearly washed-out sandcastle, and maneuver her with me. "I'm going to take some things off your hands."

Her steps slow. "Why would you do that?"

Why the heck does she seem surprised? Christ, I know the work that goes into succeeding and it's easy to tell she's struggling to do it all. "To help you out so you can study. When you take a break, I have some ideas on how I can help you relax."

Her brows pull together, and I tug her too me as a wayward football nearly hits her. "Why would you do that? What do you want in return?"

"Can't a guy help a girl out without wanting anything in return." Her gaze drops to her feet as she walks and my chest tightens. "Hey," I say to bring her attention back to me.

"I just...I don't know why you would do that." I brush my thumb over the soft skin on her wrist. "Wait, I guess I do," she says, snorting out a laugh. "Sex."

Jesus, has no one ever helped her out before? Does she always expect tit for tat? "Lanie..." Before I can say anything, a man selling hats on the beach approaches.

"Hat?" he asks, holding a long stack out to us. "Pretty lady, I have just the hat for you." He drops a pink sun hat onto her head, and she removes it quickly.

"No thanks."

"Lady, I'll give you a good deal."

She shakes her head no, and when he's about to protest, I put my hand out to stop him from dropping it back onto her head.

"No, we're good," I tell him, just as another man, one who looks to be in his mid-fifties, no doubt a guest at the resort, comes racing over. He's breathless, practically panting by the time he reaches us.

"I'll take one, actually. Mine blew away yesterday." He reaches into the front of his bathing suit, and curses under his breath. "I had cash, it must have fallen out when I went swimming. I seem to be losing everything lately." As he speaks, I smell hard liquor on his breath, and who am I to judge. The man is on vacation, and can drink what he wants, but that's probably why he's losing things.

He jerks his thumb over his shoulder. "I have to run back to my room. Can you wait?" He's about to turn, only to stop and curse. "Dammit, the wife is still sleeping and I don't want to wake her. Will you be back tomorrow?" The man swipes his hand over his balding head, burning in the morning sun.

"You need a hat today, my friend," the vendor says.

The guest turns to me, an almost pleading look on his face. "You wouldn't happen to have a twenty on you that I can borrow, would you?"

"Yeah, actually I do." Melanie's eyes go wide as I reach into my swimsuit and explain. "I was going to grab us bagels after my swim."

She shakes her head. "Brady," she murmurs, under her breath, but it's still loud enough for everyone to hear. "You can't give him money."

"I'll pay him back. I promise," the guy assures me, and I nod. When he narrows his eyes, I pull my ball cap down lower. I love my fans. I really do. Some days, however, I just want to be anonymous.

"Wait, are you..."

"Here you go," I say and hand over the cash.

"Thanks, man. Are you staying here?"

"Yeah," is all I say.

"Where can I find you?"

I glance at Melanie. "Tonight. Rooftop bar."

The guy hands the vendor the money and plops a new hat on his head. "Great, see you there."

We start walking again, and I stare at the seagulls flying overhead, circling a young boy eating a donut. I can feel Melanie's eyes on me as we walk toward the house. "What?" I ask.

"Why did you give him money? He's not going to pay you back."

I shrug. "He needed it. Did you see his forehead?"

"Do you give money to everyone who needs it?" she asks.

The truth is, I do. "Just helping out."

"You're not responsible for him," she points out, and her words hit me in the center of the chest like a hard puck. I suck in a tight breath as my muscles stiffen. "You're not responsible for anyone but yourself. I don't mean to sound harsh, Brady. It's just you're never getting that back."

She says that like she knows—has experienced it—firsthand. "He promised to repay me."

"People don't keep promises," she mumbles under her breath and keeps her head down, her focus on the sand as we walk. Her hair spills forward, veiling her face and I can't see her expression. I don't need to, really. The pain in her words was enough to let me know she'd been let down—probably many times. Goddammit, I hate that and I don't want to let her down, ever. Which once again reminds me I shouldn't be getting involved.

"Just sex, right? No commitment. No future. No promises," I say almost to myself, a reminder that I can't do more. Her head lifts and her blue eyes latch on mine. I spot a fierce determination there when she nods her head in agreement.

Okay, great. We both know exactly where we stand and what the other wants. I've always lived by those rules with women in the past, no problem. Shouldn't be a problem this time, either.

Yeah, go ahead and tell yourself that, dude.

We walk a little further, and a child about four comes racing down the beach, trips on nothing in particular and face plants in front of us. Melanie gasps and drops to her feet.

"I'm so sorry," a woman screams out and comes hurrying toward us, but Melanie already has the little girl upright and is brushing sand off her knees. "I only turned my head for a second."

Melanie laughs. "That's all it takes. I think she's perfectly fine."

"Zoe, you know you're not supposed to run off like that," the mother scolds, and takes the child into her arms to give her a big hug, clearly relieved that nothing bad happened.

"I wanted the bucket, Mommy." The mother looks toward the water, to the abandoned bucket riding the waves.

"We don't take what's not ours," the mom reminds her and looks back at Melanie. "Thank you again."

"Not a problem. She's adorable." The warm, loving look on Melanie's face curls around my heart and tugs tight. Holy crap, I don't really know much about kids, but from the longing look on Melanie's face, there's no doubt that she adores them...maybe even wants one of her own. "Are you staying here at the resort?" Melanie asks.

The mother nods. "For the weekend."

"Why don't you come up to the rooftop pool this evening? I might have something special for Zoe."

The mother gives a big smile. "That's so nice of you. What do we say, Zoe?"

Zoe glances up at Melanie with big brown eyes. "Fank you."

Melanie and the mom laugh. "I'm Gina."

"Nice to meet you, Gina. I'm Melanie." Melanie bends and taps the child's nose. "See you soon, Zoe." The mom and Zoe head back to their beach cabana, and I take Melanie's hand back in mine again.

"You're good with kids." She nods, a tender smile on her face. "You'll be a good mother."

Her demeanor changes quickly as she snorts out a laugh full of mockery. "Nope, not happening."

"Really?" I'm not sure why that surprises me. She's pretty career focused.

"I'm not bringing a child into this world." I don't tell her I totally agree—that I can't do the responsibility. "Besides, I'm too old for kids."

Okay, now that makes me laugh. "You're what, twenty-eight?"

She nods. "By the time I finish my degree, and settle into a career..."

"I don't know much about biological clocks, but I'm guessing you think yours will be done ticking by then?"

"Broken." She gives a humorless laugh. "The chance of getting pregnant goes down when you hit your thirties."

"Hey, even a broken clock is right twice a day." She rolls her eyes at me. "Well, I guess if you ever change your mind and want kids, you still have a couple good years."

She snorts again, blowing me off. I study her as she stares straight ahead. Is her clock ticking now? While not everyone is cut out to be a mother, I saw that look on her face. She wants kids.

I get the sense that it's more than school holding her back.

MELANIE

The pages before me begin to blur as I struggle to read, and I glance at my phone, knowing it's time for a break. I lift my head and from the sofa I spot Brady out on the patio, surfing rental sites on his laptop. A strange sense of warmth goes through me. I can't freaking believe he's out there searching for a place for me to live. I gave him all the necessary criteria, but the market is so tight right now, not to mention my budget. I doubt he'll be able to find me anything, and while I like my roommate, I am so ready for my own space.

Even if he does find something reasonably priced, things will be insanely tight. All extra income is going toward next year's tuition, which is due in full at the end of October. I do have my line of credit, and can probably use that until I secure a full-time job after graduation—which I have leads on. I take a deep breath and remind myself, that it's only one more year. My car, however, will have to sit idle for the time being.

As if sensing my eyes on him, his head lifts and he arches a questioning brow. I answer with a nod, letting him know I'm taking a break and he pushes to his feet, stepping back inside, laptop in hand. It's crazy what the mere sight of him does to me and for a girl who is hell bent on finding her own space, I quite enjoy sharing this place with him this weekend.

"Anything?" I ask as he walks toward me, a slow swagger that probably shouldn't turn me on but does. I give him a twice over—you know, like a once over, only I do it twice. After his jog and swim on the beach he changed into a pair of khaki shorts and a T-shirt that shows off long, lean muscles and biceps I suddenly want to take a bite out of.

I dogear the page of my textbook, and wipe my moist palms on the one sundress I brought with me. There's nothing flattering about it. I had no idea I'd have company. Yet everything in the way Brady gazes at me makes me feel beautiful again.

"Found a few leads," he informs me and my heart jumps.

"Tell me."

He sets his laptop down. "No."

"No?"

He shakes his head. "I don't want anything interfering with your studying. All focus should be on your upcoming exam." I make a move to reach for his laptop, but he slides it out of my reach. Lord knows I do everything on my own and this... handing a task over to Brady is so not like me. Then again, I'm doing a lot of things that aren't like me, but I like them. A lot.

"Fine," I grump.

He drops to his knees before me and takes my book from my

hands. "If I quiz you on what you just read, are you going to get the answers right?"

I angle my head. What is he up to? "What happens if I do get the answers right?"

He lightly toys with the short sleeves on my dress. "You'll be rewarded."

I laugh, assuming he's joking, but he pushes away, sits on the coffee table and opens the book to where I dogeared the page. He goes back about ten pages to the start of the chapter. "You started here, on chapter four?"

"Uh huh." He scans the page. "Were you a good student?" I ask. Something that looks like pain flashes in his eyes. "It's okay. I wasn't a great student growing up. I worked since I was fifteen, so it was always hard to fit in studying."

His head lifts, and the second our eyes lock, I get a sense he too had to work for everything. "There wasn't a lot of time for school," he admits. "I had hockey, and my mom..."

His words fall off and he sucks in a tight breath. "It's okay, Brady."

"She has trouble with mobility," he continues.

"I'm sorry."

"Sometimes she has a hard time walking. Her muscles seize up. She has falls." He casts me a fast glance and adds, "I think drinking is a big part of it." Shock moves over his face, giving me the sense that he'd never admitted that to himself until this very moment.

I don't touch on it, instead I ask, "You helped out a lot, huh?" If he lost his dad at eight, he must have been taking care of her for a long time.

He nods. "My uncle stays with her now."

I take his hand in mine, and not only do I sense worry in him, I sense guilt. "It's hard being away?"

"Yeah."

I lean forward and give him a soft kiss, wanting to soften his pain. "You did good for yourself, Brady. I bet they're all proud of you."

He doesn't agree, instead he answers with, "It's good I can help them all out."

He flicks the pages absently, a frown on his face like he's remembering something hard from his past. As I watch, it hits me. He takes care of his family back home—financially. He's still responsible for them. That's why he tensed up when I harshly told him he wasn't responsible for that guy on the beach. I mean, I guess it's okay to feel responsible for your family, especially when times are hard, which they seem to be in Newfoundland. Why then, do I think there is more going on here?

I'm about to ask, but in the blink of an eye, his playful demeanor returns, disguising the emotions he doesn't want me to see. "Are you ready to be quizzed, little Lanie?"

I resist the urge to press. He's done with this conversation, and is making it clear he wants to move on. "Bring it," I say and lean back on the sofa.

He reads a paragraph, and starts listing off medical conditions. "Okay, what's the diagnosis for that?" he asks.

I quickly blurt out the answer. "Bipolar."

"Very good." He reads the next paragraph.

"Wait, what's my reward? I got it right."

"So, you did."

He sets the book down, drops to his knees and puts his hand behind my head. He pulls my mouth to his as he leans in and gives me a deep, hard kiss that steals my breath. After he breaks it, he sits back on the coffee table and I take a few panting breaths.

"Okay, Brady, how the heck am I supposed to think after that?"

He winks at me. "That's just going to make it more challenging, and I know you're not afraid of a challenge."

I fan my hand in front of my face. "What makes you say that?"

"You just told me you started work at fifteen, and I see how hard you work at the resort and you're doing your master's degree at the same time. That's challenging and you have all my respect, babe."

My heart soars. I like that he sees that in me, and respects what I'm doing. "Okay, next question." Under my breath I murmur, "Can't wait to see what my reward is when I get it right."

He wags his brows and adjusts the bulge in his shorts. "I'm not going to make this easy on you."

"I think it's going to be *hard* for both of us."

He laughs and asks me another question. I get it right, and pucker my lips. He doesn't go for them, however. Nope, He drops to his knees, puts his hands on my sides, and lightly rubs my nipples through my dress.

"God, Brady, really?"

"Hard," he reminds me and I let my head fall back as a groan crawls out of my throat.

"Yes, hard," I agree. He leans in and presses his mouth to one nipple through the fabric of my dress. His hot breath seeps through the thin material and washes over my nipple. He inches back, and I glance down at the damp spot he left behind. "You're getting me wet." He chuckles and that's when I realize what I said. I roll my eyes at him. "You know what I mean."

He puts his hands on my thighs. "You're telling me you're not getting wet."

"No, I'm not telling you that."

He laughs and sits back on the coffee table, leaving me a quivering mess on the sofa. He flips the page, and looking completely unaffected he reads the next question. I almost don't answer correctly. The man is killing me here. But because I'm an overachiever and hate to be wrong, I give the correct answer, and let's face it, I really want to see what my reward is.

"Very good, Lanie."

He sinks back to the floor, and his big, warm hands slide up my thighs and under my sundress. I take a gulping breath and widen my legs to give him better access to the needy spot that wants his attention.

"Let's see if you were telling me the truth."

I sink back into the sofa. "I always tell the truth," I murmur as he tugs my panties to the side and lightly runs his finger over my hot sex. "Brady..."

"Mmm, so nice and wet for me. I'm going to have to have a taste, Lanie."

"Yes, please." I open my eyes as he pushes a finger inside me. I lift my hips as he slowly moves his finger in and out. God, that feels so damn good. His thumb toys with my clit as he slowly, methodically fucks me with his finger, and just when my entire body flushes, he pulls out and sits back on the coffee table.

"Are you kidding me right now?" I huff.

"No, babe. We have to get through this chapter."

"Brady," I groan.

"One more question." Again, looking unaffected, even though the bulge in his pants tells a different story, he asks me a question and I blurt out the answer, desperate for him to be between my legs. "Very good," he tells me and sets the book aside. A little squeal of joy crawls out of my throat as he drops again, his fingers seeking my panties.

He grips them, and quickly pulls them off, but instead of tossing them aside, he shoves them into his pocket like they're a souvenir, and it oddly arouses me.

I grab the hem of my dress and pull it up, exposing my hot, needy pussy to him. He growls with pleasure as he takes in my pink dampness. "What was that you said about needing a taste?"

His breath is warm on my skin and vibrates through me as he grips my legs to widen them more, and gives me a wicked grin before he covers my sex with his mouth.

"Yes," I cry out and lace my fingers through his hair. He licks me, circles the soft blade of his tongue around my clit, until

I'm panting and writhing, and delirious with want. "Brady…" I beg, and he answers my cries by sliding a thick finger inside me. I move, riding his finger as he sucks my swollen clit into his mouth, nibbling and biting until I'm a hot freaking mess. He gifts me with a second finger for a snug fit as the dual pleasure of his fingers inside me and his mouth on my clit instantly push me over the edge.

"Fuck yeah," he murmurs as my liquid arousal spills from my body. He groans as he unceremoniously eats at me, licking and drinking every drop like I'm the best thing he's ever tasted. I work to breathe as he devours me. After a moment, his head lifts and intense eyes lock on mine. He pops the button on his khakis and pulls out his gorgeous hard cock.

I reach for him, take him into my hands and he closes his over mine as I stroke the long length of him. "My turn," I say.

He arches a brow, confused and I chuckle. "I get to ask a question, and if you get it right, you get rewarded."

"Yeah, okay," he huffs out, like breathing is now a chore. He glances at my book for a second. "I don't really know much about psychology."

"My question has nothing to do with my course."

"Ask," he grumbles as he squeezes my hand around his dick, working it harder.

I blow a strand of hair from my damp forehead. "Do you want to fuck me?"

He grunts. "Yeah, I do."

"That's the right answer," I say and stand, pulling on him so he'll stand with me. He pushes up to his full height, and I turn him until the backs of his knees are hitting the cushions.

Confusion moves over his face, but it disappears quickly when I give him a shove. He falls onto the cushions, and I hold my dress up and climb over him.

I reach down, and grip his cock, and he groans as I position him at my entrance. His fingers tighten around my sides, as I lower myself, taking every inch of him into my needy body.

"Lanie," he groans as I sink down until he's hitting my cervix in the most delicious ways. "You are so hot and tight. I'm not going to fucking last."

I lift myself up, and drop back down again, and our groans mingle. I wiggle and rotate my hips, wanting everything he has and then some. Honest to God, as he fills me, I consider my sanity. Nothing has ever felt this good before, which begs the question, why the hell did I wait so long to sleep with him? I can't come up with the answer right now and I don't much care. Not when Brady is gripping me tighter and taking control of my body, lifting me up and pulling me back down onto his steel cock.

I cup his cheeks and find his mouth, our tongues tangling and tasting as we come together as one. I break the kiss and glance down, needing to watch the way he's impaling me, and taking me to heights I've never know before I met him.

"Brady, I don't ever want to stop doing this," I cry out without thinking it through.

"Same, Lanie." He growls, leans forward and nibbles my nipple through my dress, and I tug my dress down, offering him my breasts. "That's more like it." He sucks my nipples, his mouth going from one to the other as he lifts me, and pulls me back down again.

I grind against him, and slip a hand between my legs to stroke my clit.

My nipple slips from his mouth as he dips his head to see me play with my clit. "Yeah, baby. Rub yourself for me. That is so fucking hot."

My finger slicks over my wet clit as he impales me, each thrust shattering me just a little bit more. He increases the pace as we each chase release and the second he pulls me down, his crown hitting my cervix hard, I shatter around him.

His eyes meet mine and briefly close as I soak his cock. "Fuck yeah." His fingers bite harder into my hips and he holds me down on him as he jerks upward with his hips. A second later, his head rolls back as he tumbles into orgasm. "Lanie. Fuck."

I suck in air, panting as his cock swells inside me, his liquid release warming me from the inside out. I fall forward, and rest my forehead against his as he continues to pulse. His arms snake around my back, a soft caress as he pulls me against him.

We hold onto one another until our breathing levels out. Body lethargic, and happy from my orgasmic bliss, I'm about to ask him if he wants to take a fast afternoon nap, but my words die an abrupt death, when his now cool hands grip my shoulders, to straighten me.

The second I see the stricken look on his face, blood rushes back into my brain, and I realize what we've done.

"Oh no."

"I'm on the pill," Melanie blurts out.

My stalled heart starts beating again as she climbs off my body, my cock sliding from her slick, warm channel. "I always use a condom."

Her dress falls over her thighs as she stands, her flushed cheeks paling slightly. "I don't know what I was thinking. I'm sorry, Brady."

"We both got carried away." Hell, this isn't all on her. I hold responsibility for it too.

"Yeah, but that's never happened to me before."

"Same," I tell her, not sure if that's a good thing or a bad. "You're on the pill," I mumble, mostly to myself.

"I am. It helps regulate my periods," she says, and I meet her troubled gaze as she takes a step back, stopping when her legs hit the coffee table. Dammit, I didn't mean to sound like I was challenging that, or that I didn't believe her. I stand, shove my dick back into my boxers and pull her to me.

She's stiff at first, and I rub her back. Her body softens against mine and I whisper, "It's all good." I press my mouth to her ear. "I'm clean, if you're worried about that. Like I said, I always use a condom."

"I'm clean too."

I chuckle lightly. "Dammit, now I know why that felt so incredible. Skin on skin." I'm not sure if that's the reason, though. I think it felt incredible because it was with this amazing woman.

"It was pretty nice."

I laugh, and inch back. "Nice? Nice enough that you said you never wanted to stop doing it." I take in the pink on her cheeks.

She glances away, almost sheepish. "I did say that, didn't I?"

"Did you mean it?"

"Well yeah. I mean, until your pre-season kicks in."

"Right." I can't tell whether I'm relieved or not by that. The truth is I like her, and I want to keep doing it too. I just hope that I'll have worked her out of my system by the time pre-season does start. She swallows, and it sounds tortured. "Water?"

"Yes please."

I give her backside a tap. "Why don't you get started on your next chapter?"

She stretches her arms out. "I think I'll have a fast shower first. Join me?"

I laugh. "If I join you, it won't be a fast shower, and you have studying to do."

"Also, I might need to make a trip back to my place. It's possible I've run out of panties."

I grin, and reach around to my back pocket, tapping the panties I stole. "You don't need panties this weekend, Lanie."

She laughs and kisses me, and I'm happy that the tension from earlier has dissipated. Christ, not once have I forgotten to use a condom. Thank God she's on the pill, or we'd be running to the drug store. I will never bring a child into this world. I mean, what if something happened and I couldn't be there for them. Nope, not going there.

"Are you okay?" Melanie asks, and I shake off bad memories. I tap her ass again. "Let me get you a drink before you shower." I start toward the kitchen and my phone rings. The familiar chime is a reminder that I forgot to call my mother back, and that's her now. My muscles stiffen as I pick up my phone and slide my finger across the screen. I catch Melanie's curious gaze as I walk into the kitchen.

"Hey," I say as I answer.

"I've been calling." Mom's voice is a bit slurry. No doubt from all the pain meds...mixed with alcohol.

"Yeah, sorry. Been busy."

"Too busy for your own mother?"

"No, uh. Just had some things to take care of." I grab a bottle of water from the fridge, and find Melanie standing in the doorway. I hand it to her and give a nod when she gazes at me, her eyes questioning if I'm okay.

"Jeez, ducky. Thought you died on me."

"No, just ah..." Melanie takes the water and disappears down the hall. "How are you feeling?" That question sets Mom off on a litany of aches and pains she's currently experiencing. "I'm going to need more money, Brady."

"What for?" I ask.

"The water heater is gone, and you know I don't have any extra cash laying around."

Naturally I'm going to give her the money, but I was sure there was a leak just last year and it was replaced. "Didn't you just replace that last year?"

"Are you calling me a liar?"

"No, of course not." I walk to the patio and glance out at the busy beach. "How much?"

"A few thousand." Something bangs in the background and my uncle's curses come through the phone. "Your cousin Bethany needs to get some new skates for the kids." I don't answer right away, my gaze on the guy trying to windsurf with no wind, which results in Mom saying, "You know times are tight here. It's not like I'm spending it on anything frivolous. If I had any of your father's life insurance money left..."

"Carl is still out of work?" For as long as I've known Bethany's husband Carl, he's been out of work. Times are tough in Newfoundland, that's for sure.

"Not much for him here in Paradise."

"No, you're right, and kids do need new skates every year." I remember one year when I needed two new pairs. That was when I was going through a crazy growth spurt.

"You were lucky we had the money to buy them."

"True," I say, feeling guilty that I should be grateful, even though I don't feel all that lucky. Except when I'm with, Melanie. That's when I feel lucky. Shit.

I click open the patio door and swallow down the emotions before they affect my voice. I don't need to be told to stop being a pussy. "I'll send money for skates."

Down the hall the shower turns on, and I shift toward the sound. "You'll send it today?" Mom asks.

"Yeah, sure." I walk back to the kitchen to get my own water.

"You might want to throw in a couple extra thousand. The kids will need school supplies and things too, and Aunt Ester could use a few things."

I nod even though she can't see me. "Pre-season starts in a couple weeks," I say, for lack of anything else.

"You're keeping yourself fit and healthy." Her tone holds accusation, and I stand up a bit straighter.

"Of course."

"You know you can't afford to slack off, b'y. I put everything into your career."

Actually, I put everything into my career. The work, the time, the sacrifices... Dad's death paid for it, sure, but I'd rather have him alive. "Yeah."

"I'll be checking my account, then."

Her words hold closure, signifying the end of our conversation. "Okay, bye." I toss my phone onto the counter, the knot in my stomach tightening. I stand there for a second, taking a couple of deep breaths, until the sound of water running draws me toward it.

I walk down the hall, tearing my T-shirt off as I go. I'm not going to fuck Melanie again. I just want to hold her tight. The room is steamy when I enter, and since I don't want to scare her, I call out to her.

"Need a hand?"

The glass door slides open and she peeks out. "What about my studying?"

Fuck. "Right." I take a step back and she angles her head.

"Are you okay?"

"Sure, fine." I laugh and blow the whole thing off, even though my insides are still wound tight. "Just thought I could use a shower."

Silence hangs heavy for a second and then she holds her hand out to me. "Get in here, Coddy."

A crazy sense of relief washes through me. I kick my pants off and climb into the shower, letting the hot spray soothe me. I avoid her gaze. She's a smart woman, and I don't want her seeing through me. She doesn't speak, or ask me about my call, or why I'm suddenly so fucking needy. Instead, she picks up the soap, lathers her hands and twirls one finger.

I turn beneath the spray, lifting my face to the rain shower nozzle and she lathers my back. "That's nice."

"No one has ever washed your back before?"

I decide to be honest since honesty is important to her. "No. You?"

Her soft chuckle curls around me, and as it soothes my soul, I can't help but wonder why she finds that question so amusing. "No."

"How about we change that." I turn, and squirt the liquid soap into my hands. It's so odd, I was just inside her, but being here in the shower, touching her softly. I don't know...it somehow feels more intimate. What the fuck is happening to me? If I want to make it in this world, I need to remain hard and detached. If I let emotions in, it could fuck up my head and my game, and then how could I take care of those counting on me?

"Brady..."

I slowly slide my slick hands over her tiny frame, and lift her arms so I can run my fingers up her sides. She quivers as I touch her. "Yeah."

"Who were you talking to? If you don't mind me asking. If you do, you don't have to answer. I'm only asking because you seemed upset."

I slide my hands around her body and pull her against my chest. I put my mouth on the side of her neck and my breathing is rough, uneven against her flesh as I give her a soft kiss. "It was my mother."

"Okay."

We don't move, we just stay still with our bodies fused, and she doesn't press. Honestly, I'm grateful she's not digging into my past. My childhood and life back home isn't something I talk about. So why the hell am I opening my mouth, unraveling like the frayed pair of pajama shorts she wore last night? "Water heater is broken, and my cousin's kids both need new skates. They need me to send money."

Her body stiffens and I curse myself. What the hell is wrong with me? "It's nice of you to get them skates." I don't answer and she continues. "I can see why you were upset. A broken water heater is no fun."

"Nope, having no hot water is no fun at all. It'll definitely need to be fixed before it gets cold." I work to inject playfulness in my voice, though it's really fucking hard right now. "You can't be in Newfoundland in the winter with no hot water."

She mocks a shiver. "I wouldn't want to be anywhere without hot water."

I chuckle. "True."

"When I get my own place, I'm going to have the longest showers. I can't do that in my shared apartment because we run out of hot water was too fast."

I run my hands around her body, and soap her stomach. Her head falls back against my shoulder, and our bodies meld together. I put my mouth near her ear as I think about long showers. "Sounds luxurious."

"Do you want to own your own place someday?"

It's a simple, innocent question, so my stomach shouldn't be coiling like a snake about to attack. But owning my own place means one more thing I'm responsible for. That, and I'm afraid to spend the money. What if a family member needs help and I'm unable to be there for them?

"Big house on Beacon Hill," she teases. "Up there with all the other hockey players."

"Why would I want that when I can run on the beach here every morning?" She angles her head like she's not quite buying that. "Besides, I'm only one person. I'd get lost in a big place on

Beacon Hill." I understand what she's hinting at, though. Noah and Brighton's family is expanding, and they're not always going to want me in the suite across the hall. I'm sure they'll be breaking down walls and renovating to make it one big place.

"You help out a lot." My brain, still processing Beacon Hill, works to catch up as she adds, "With your family back in Newfoundland. You've been the man around the house for a long time, even though it's been a long time since you've actually lived in your childhood house."

Again, another simple, innocent statement, but it hits my gut like a runaway slap shot, and I nearly bend forward. "Yeah."

"What would they do without you?"

My head drops, weighed down with worry, as my heart pounds against her back. She turns in my arms, her eyes piercing mine, searching my face with concern. This woman is far too astute for me, so I try to drag a laugh up from the pit of my stomach, but it doesn't make it to my lips.

"That's not going to happen," I push out, the seriousness and conviction in my tone startling Lanie—and myself. But Christ, it's not going to happen. Can't. While I continually tell myself that like it's law, it's what I worry about most— what keeps me up at night.

One soft palm settles on my cheek. "Brady. I'm just saying people do find a way to manage on their own. Trust me on this."

As water pours down on me, something inside me bubbles over, spills from a well that has been filling up with no relief valve to release the excess pressure, and before I can stop myself, I begin, "I had an accident." Her eyes narrow in on me as trauma from my past grips me like a tight belt around my chest and squeezes the air from my lungs. "I was just a stupid teen." I laugh as some childhood learned response forces me to do so, and I'm about to change the subject—because what the fuck am I doing—but Melanie puts both arms around me and holds tight. Jesus, her support weakens me and strengthens me at the same time, so instead of joking around, I continue. "I was sixteen. New license. Stupid kid stuff down at the abandoned quarry."

"You were hurt," she states, her voice breaking slightly, and it's that break and everything in those three words that lets me know she realizes it wasn't just the accident that hurt me.

"I banged my head on the steering wheel and blacked out."

She puts her hand on my chest, and my heart pounds against her soft palm. Her gaze says it all as she watches me carefully. She knows I've been hurt and I'm not telling the entire truth. Not being honest which is the only thing she's ever asked of me. "Brady...it's okay."

Her soft understanding tone has me uttering, "My mom had a fall that day. She was taken to the hospital by neighbors who finally found her. Everyone had tried to get a hold of me, but I had wrapped my car around a tree and my buddy and I were knocked out cold. We stayed like that until some guy out walking his dog found us and called an ambulance."

The hard quiver going through her, reverberates through me. "That's horrifying. I can't even imagine how frightened you must have been." As she speaks, I shut my eyes as painful memories explode in my brain, flashing like bright lightning on a dark rainy night. "Your buddy...was he...okay? Nothing more than getting knocked out?"

"We both had concussions, but nothing broken." As I speak, it's strange. There's a weird kind of relief inside me, the band around my chest, which has constantly constricted my lungs, has loosened a tiny bit.

"Thank God." Her hands move gently over my back. "Your mom and the neighbors must have been worried sick when they couldn't reach you."

I swallow against a painful throat. "No...my mother."

She presses a light kiss to my chest, right around the vicinity of my heart. "You said she had a fall."

"Yeah, it was a bad one. She was hanging clothes on the line, and tumbled. We live near a rocky cliff." A hard quiver grips me, and I shake. Melanie holds me tighter, her touch comforting. Honest to fuck, has anyone ever held me like this before? No, because I never would have allowed it. "I was supposed to be there for her."

Melanie inches back slightly, her arms still around me. Strands of wet hair stick to her forehead, and I pick it up and move it. "You were sixteen."

"Yeah." So, she gets it. A cold shiver wracks my body, despite the hot water pouring over me. "I was sixteen and stupid and irresponsible when I was supposed to be watching my mother. I don't know what I was thinking. I should have been home. If something worse had happened to me..."

"No wait, Brady." Her voice holds a measure of outrage that she seems to be trying to control as she shakes her head. "You were sixteen being sixteen, thinking with a sixteen-year-old brain."

"Yeah, but I shouldn't have been. I was supposed to hang the laundry. After Dad died..." I swallow as the words burn in my esophagus and lodge in the back of my throat.

"Brady, you could have killed yourself and what I'm hearing is that you were in *trouble* because your mother had a fall, and you weren't there to help her."

"I didn't say that." At least, I don't think I did. But I could be wrong. Maybe no one caring about me that day hurt a little. Or a lot.

"You said it, just not in words." She grips my shoulders and I stiffen. "You were sixteen. Parents are responsible for their children when they're sixteen. Not vice versa." Under her breath she adds, "At least, they should be." I take in the frown on her forehead, the hurt and fury in her eyes and something tells me she's talking from experience—and not the kind learned in textbooks. "Kids shouldn't be responsible for their parents at that age and what I'm hearing, Brady, is you were in trouble for getting into a car accident and nearly killing yourself, because if you killed yourself, you wouldn't be there for your mother." I stare at her as her words bounce around inside my brain. "Do you have any idea how messed up that is?"

I come to my mother's defense. "She'd used Dad's life insurance for my hockey." Fuck, where would I be without it. Back in Newfoundland, trying to make ends meet like the rest of them.

She blinks once, twice, and looks at me like that concussion might have done more damage than I'm letting on. As we stare at one another, the water cools my already chilled body. "Speaking of hot water...we're running out."

She backs up. "Yeah, we are."

I turn around and shut off the tap before it's icy cold. I reach out and grab the big towel on the hook.

"Sorry, I didn't put one there for you. Didn't know you'd be joining me."

I shake out the towel and wrap it around my body, and pull her against me. "We can share. It's big enough for the both of us." She wiggles against me. "Lanie."

"Yeah."

We step from the shower, and I hold her tight. "Who didn't keep their promises?

10

MELANIE

The sun is still high in the sky as I pour a rum and coke into a glass and take in all the patrons at the rooftop bar. My gaze slides to Brady, who is chatting with Conner, one of his closest friends on the team. I've met Conner a couple of times and he seems nice enough. He's always polite when he orders a drink and tips well. He usually hangs out with his sister-in-law, Dani. I used to think that was odd, until I learned that his brother—Dani's husband—died in a car accident a couple of years ago. Maybe they need each other and it helps the healing process.

While I have no idea what they're talking about, I do note the way Conner's gaze keeps straying to me, and the way he keeps whacking Brady and laughing like they're sharing an inside joke. Brady, however, isn't laughing and that's odd for him when he's in a crowded room. The man loves to be the center of attention. He never stands there, scrubbing a hand over his chin his eyes cast downward like he's the butt of a joke, when he's normally the joker. A strange uneasy thread of worry works its way through my body as I tear my gaze away.

"Hi Melanie," Zoe says as she and her mother come up to the bar.

I lean over the counter. "Why hello, Zoe." I smile at Gina. "Can I make you a drink?"

"I'd love a strawberry daiquiri."

"Two daiquiris coming up." I wink at her. "One virgin."

I go to work on the drinks and drop a cute umbrella into Zoe's. I step from behind the counter, hand Gina her drink and drop to my knees to give Zoe hers. Her eyes go wide with excitement and just seeing the happiness on her face fills my heart with joy, but it hurts just as much, which is probably why my conversation with Brady is jumping to the forefront of my brain. Maybe I do want kids. I just don't want to bring them into this world.

"Mommy, an umbrella!" She takes it from her drink and holds it over her head and we all giggle. That's when I feel Brady's eyes on me, and I lift my head to find him watching, all the while the guys around him are laughing and joking, but his sole focus is on me, and I momentarily forget how to breathe.

"I have something for you," Gina says.

I stand to my full height. "What, are you kidding? Why would you do that?"

"To thank you for this morning."

She reaches into her purse and pulls out a gift card.

I stare at it and read the bold lettering. *The Nook.*

"It's a small café. I'd love to treat you and your husband for lunch."

Husband.

My gaze strays to Brady again and I try not to sound breathless when I respond. "Oh, he's just a friend."

"Sorry, I thought...you two seemed more."

"It's okay." I see Brady turn from me when Conner puts his hand on his shoulder.

"Well, I'd like to treat you and whoever you'd like to bring, to lunch."

What's the catch? "Why would you—"

She shrugs. "I actually inherited the place from an uncle I never knew." Her eyes go wide. "Crazy, right?" I node in agreement. "Anyway, I'm pretty new to this town and learning my way around. It's not easy meeting people when you're a single mom. I just thought—"

"I would love to come," I tell her, understanding that the catch is she wants to meet people and possibly be friends.

"Great, I look forward to it. How much for the drinks?"

"On the house and I have a little something special for Zoe." Zoe, who is busy playing with her umbrella, stops when she hears her name. I step back behind the bar and grab the plastic bucket and shovel I picked up for her today at the gift shop. I get an employee discount, so it was pretty cheap and the smile on the little girl's face as I hand it to her...priceless.

"I love it. Fank you."

Gina rubs the top of Zoe's head and gives me a grateful smile. "That's so kind of you."

"My pleasure."

"I really look forward to seeing you at the café. Bring a friend."

"Will do."

She steps away and I go back behind the counter, nodding to one of the hockey players when he comes up and gestures to me for three beers. I pour off three draft beers and slide them to him. He pays and I wipe the counter down as more players fill the rooftop bar.

Deanna, my server for the night, drops her tray onto the bar and hands me a list with drinks. "Busy night." She turns to take in the players and a moan catches in her throat. "What do you think of Conner?"

I glance at Conner as he talks to some random girl, as Dani engages Gunther in conversation. "You like him?"

She grins at me. "He's cute."

I shrug. "I guess if you're into guys like that."

"Oh yeah, which one do you like?"

"None of them," I tell her.

"Girl, you must be made of ice because there are plenty of hotties to pick from." She arches one brow. "Maybe you should pick one, you know, to help melt that ice."

I chuckle as I fill her drink order. "I'm good."

"Maybe, but if you took one of those guys home, you'd be great." She's not wrong, and I plan to do just that, but that's my little secret. "He's not with that girl, is he?"

"Dani, you mean?"

"Is that her name?" She watches the two. "He treats her like a sister, but she barely leaves his side, especially when there are so many hot players here."

"He treats her like a sister because she's his sister-in-law."

"Ah, okay." With a little extra wiggle in her hips, she walks away with her tray and I smile as the guys all slap each other on the back, and I have to say I do enjoy their comradery. This has become a popular spot for them all to hang out since Noah bought the place and I don't hate it, because all the tips are going to help pay for next semester.

A loud laugh that's very familiar curls around me and I lift my gaze and spot Brady, Conner and Gunther all joking—the random girl is now chatting with Theo. Once again, the guys keep casting glances my way. What the hell are they talking about now, and why—although Brady is laughing along—does whatever they're saying seems to be rubbing him the wrong way? I can tell by his body language that something isn't sitting well with him.

I grab the ice and try not to think about whatever it is they're talking about, because really, it's not my business. I just hope the inside joke isn't about me, although I don't know why it would be. I don't think Brady is the kind of guy to kiss and tell, and now that I've gotten to know him better, I can see a whole new side to him. The man is tortured, has far too many demons for a guy his age, and has people in his life who've been taking advantage of him for far too long.

I swallow down my own pain as I consider the way I dismissed his question after our shower today. He opened up to me, told me something very private about his past, and I simply shut him down. Yeah, I used my studying as an excuse, and he backed right off, because he knows college is important to me. Still, my brush off had to sting a bit, after he shared a big part of his life with me.

The problem is, though, Brady can't see what's going on in his own backyard, so to speak. I get that he wants to help his family and that's admirable. If you ask me, and no one really is, I'd say hockey was money in the bank for his family. An investment in Brady so he could continue to take care of them all into the future. I didn't say that to him, of course. I didn't want to hurt him.

Soon enough, it's dark out, the setting sun sending the kids home for the night, and now the adults are pouring onto the rooftop. Phones are pulled from pockets and pool bags as guests want their pictures taken with the guys, and the single girls, and not so single ones, are all over the guys. I turn my head and try not to let it bother me. It shouldn't bother me. I've seen enough of it since Noah bought the resort. I wasn't, however, banging and poking with Brady until now. I really have no right to be jealous. He's not mine. I'm not his. We're simply playing house until the end of the weekend and while we said we'd do this until he went off to the pre-season, I'm sure once I find my own place, that plan will be out the window. That's probably for the best.

The tiki lights around me light up, as well as the lights in the pool as a man walks up to the bar and orders a beer. I pour him a draft as he smiles at me, grinning the whole time. I slide it to him. "Here you go."

He adjusts his hat, and that's when I place him. He gestures with a nod over his shoulder. "I knew it was Brady Fisher."

I chuckle. "He does stand out, doesn't he?"

"People are getting their pictures with him. Do you think he'd mind? He didn't seem to want the attention this afternoon."

This afternoon he was with me...and was quite different from the showboat he's presenting tonight.

I grin, liking that he wanted our time together to be private and real, where he wasn't loud and obnoxious. Maybe that's why this man didn't recognize him at first. "Looks like he's enjoying himself over there. I'm sure he won't mind at all."

"I still owe him twenty."

I nod, somewhat surprised, but maybe not so surprised at all. He can't very well walk up and ask for a picture when he owes money. There's always a catch.

He takes his drink and leaves me a tip. I pocket it. "Thanks, and enjoy your evening."

He saunters over to Brady, who doesn't seem surprised to see him at all. I laugh. While the man is constantly taken advantage of, he still has faith in mankind and I don't know if that's a good thing or a naïve thing. All I know is that I don't ever plan to be duped again.

Brady lifts his head and catches my eyes, and he has a smirk on his face and I just shake my head in response. He goes back to the pictures, having fun, and I go back to bartending. About thirty minutes later, he saunters up to the bar, a crisp twenty in his hand.

He snaps it. "See, not everyone breaks their promises."

"Guess not." I keep my opinion on it to myself.

"What?"

"Nothing."

I pour him a beer and slide it across the bar. "Hey, I saw the smile on Zoe's face when you gave her the umbrella. That was pretty cute."

"Yeah, she really liked it." I pull the card from my pocket. "Look what Gina gave me." I hold it out and he takes it. "It's a gift card to her café," I explain. "Apparently, she's new here and inherited a café. I'm curious to check it out."

"That was really nice of her."

I grab a rag and wipe a dripping tap. "She's looking for new friends."

He angles his head. "You think that's why she invited you?"

"That, or for helping her daughter out."

He goes quiet for a moment, and I can almost feel him trying to tunnel into my brain. "You think everything has a catch, a price attached, don't you?"

I laugh, but it's cool and bitter. "Are you saying it doesn't?"

He holds out the twenty-dollar bill again. "He paid me back. Didn't break his promise."

"He did take lots of pictures with you."

"Lots of people do. Doesn't mean they want anything from me. They're just happy to get pictures with the players they love." I make a snorting noise and he continues. "Not everything has a catch, Lanie."

"Whatever you say, Coddy." I laugh and add, "She thought you were my husband." I take a fast look at his face to gauge his reaction, and when his brows pull together, I laugh and add, "Ludicrous, right?"

"Yeah, ludicrous," he agrees and suddenly it doesn't sound so funny anymore.

"Coddy, get over here. We're going to do cannon balls," Theo bellows.

Jaw tight, face sober and unamused, he murmurs, "Jesus."

"Not into cannon balls?" I ask.

He grunts. "That guy gets on my nerves."

"I'm pretty sure it was just last month you were the ringleader for cannon balls." My words instantly trigger a reaction in him. His face changes from serious and reflective to jovial, and playful.

"Yeah, maybe too much sun today. Nothing that a beer can't fix." He picks up his beer and I expect him to down it, but instead he takes a sip and walks away. He reaches his friends and sets his beer on a table, forgotten, and goes to the end of the pool and does a cannon ball. I chuckle as everyone watching yells as he splashes them.

He surfaces and bets his friends that they can't make a bigger splash and I just shake my head at his antics. Fun and loud Brady. Everything I've seen over the last couple of months and have come to expect from him. *But is it, though, Melanie?* As that question fills me with more questions, my mind goes back to the softness about this man, the seriousness in his body, his face and actions when he says or does certain things. Hell, he couldn't hide that seriousness when he talked about his family. At one point, I thought he was going to break down, and maybe that's exactly what he needs.

The night drones on, and soon enough it's closing time, and the guests make their way to their rooms or their vehicles to drive home. I catch a glimpse of Brady, some girl wrapped all around him as he practically carries her drunk ass down the stairs.

I try to push down my apprehension as I remind myself we're not exclusive. We said we'd bang and poke until the pre-season. We didn't say that we wouldn't see other people. Honestly though, I'm not sure I want that. I can't be with a man when he's also with other people. As my stomach sinks into my toes, Deanna drops her tray onto the counter.

"This place is a mess."

"You go on home, I'll clean up." Her eyes practically bulge out of her head.

"Are you serious?"

I nod, needing time alone with my thoughts, and the strange ache in my chest. That ache is there because I know what I have to do—end it with Brady. I can't be doing this bang and poke with him when he's with other women.

Is that the real reason, girl?

Okay, maybe I can't do it because I'm beginning to really like him—especially the side he presents to me when we're alone.

Deanna is quick to take me up on my offer. She leaves, and I shut and lock the gate leading to the rooftop and begin to clean up.

I pick up empty drink glasses and a few that are still full, like the one Brady left on the table after I poured it for him. Maybe he doesn't like beer. I usually see him with one in his hand. I never stopped to think if he was drinking it or not. Legs tired and needing to get to bed early so I can bus back to my place tomorrow—I really hope my roommate's boyfriend is gone—I finish cleaning up.

Once I'm done, I untie my apron and toss it over my shoulder. I snatch up my purse from under the counter and walk toward the gate as the quiet of the night, along with the surf far below wraps around my shaky soul. I reach the gate and when I see a big, dark figure on the other side, I nearly jump out of my skin.

"Hey, it's just me," Brady says quickly, his voice is soft, full of comfort, and my insides settle.

"What are you doing here?" I ask, as he stands outside the latched gate, heat and strength radiating from him.

His eyes fixate on my mouth and I wet my lips. "Thought I'd walk you home." Beneath the moonlight I catch his sexy grin and unwanted emotions sweep through me. God, I could lose myself in this man if I'm not careful. My gaze strays to his mouth, dying for his lips to claim me again. That's when I remember the girl who was snaked around him earlier.

"Didn't you already walk someone home?" Dammit, I didn't mean to sound so petty and jealous. The last thing I want is for him to think I'm falling for him.

Amusement dances on his face. "Sounds like someone is jealous."

I glance down, and run my fingers through my hair, pushing the loose strands from my forehead. "Brady, I can't—"

"I can't either," he responds quickly, cutting me off as my gaze flies back to his, to take in the dead seriousness.

"You can't what?"

"I can't be with another girl when I have a woman like you in my bed. I want to be with you and only you. I want to take you to my bed...want to take care of you, Lanie." He squares his shoulder with intent, and there's nothing about his body language that suggests he's joking. I really truly love this side of him. *Like.* I mean I really truly *like* this quiet, almost nurturing side of him. I swallow the lump in my throat as he continues. "She was drunk. All I did was make sure she got home safely. I'm sure they assumed I took her home and fucked her, but she was drunk, and I don't do drunk girls. Even if she wasn't drunk, Lanie. I wanted to be back here with you."

A bubble of happiness hugs me. "Oh."

He pokes his chest before pointing at me through the gate. "You and me. Until the pre-season. No one else."

"Okay," I manage to get out.

"Now are you going to open this gate and let me take you home?"

"I'm quite capable of finding my own way home. I've been taking care of myself for a very long time now."

"I know, but..."

"What's the catch, Coddy?" I grin, knowing the catch is he wants me in his bed, and I want that too.

He glances around. "Bad neighborhood."

It's not. We both know it, but I do love this protective side of him. As his warmth envelops me, I tease, "Maybe just bad *neighbor.*"

"Hey, I resent that," he teases.

"Why, maybe I like bad." I open the gate and let him in. He closes it behind him and his big presence overwhelms me as he pulls me to his body. His warm scent fills my senses and as I breathe him in, he dips his head and kisses me. I moan into his mouth, loving the taste of him.

"You want bad tonight, Lanie?"

Moaning something unintelligible, I sway into his touch, and my body warms as his erection presses hard against me. I kind of love how fast this man gets aroused around me. Who am I to talk? I'm burning from the inside out. His hand slides down my body and cups my ass. He gives it a squeeze as the automatic lights in the pool turn off for the night. Darkness envelops us, and all kinds of wicked ideas bounce around inside my brain—like getting him naked here at the rooftop pool and having my way with him.

Yes, it's true. We had sex earlier, but this has easily become my addiction. I want more, and I want it now. *Oh girl, you need to be careful.*

"I'm not used to people waiting for me," I whisper, actually loving that he came here to walk me home as a strange new closeness to this man fills every cell in my body.

His snort is full of derision. "And here I am completely used to people waiting for me. Everywhere. All the time."

My chest tightens, another hint of jealousy I shouldn't be feeling creeping in and squeezing like an invisible band. Until I realize he's most likely talking about his family, who all seem to count on him. While he might be loud and the life of the party, he never had a real childhood and I'm guessing he acts out now to make up for it. Either that or he's loud at parties simply to hide who he really is, what he's really feeling. My heart lurches at that thought. Is that what's going on?

Does Brady Fisher hide his emotions behind a shield of sarcasm and jokes? I'm not sure. But I do know that beneath the layers, there's real softness there, and that he's way more in control of himself and his life here in Boston than he lets on. Honestly, the man is a conundrum, one for the textbooks, for sure.

"I guess we're different like that," he murmurs.

"We might have more in common than you think."

"That's right, we both have roommates who fuck like bunnies." His laugh is light, and it eases some of the tension inside me.

"Right. Mine bangs like bricks in a dryer," I agree, even though I'm talking about our upbringing. Sure, he was raised in Newfoundland without a father and a needy family. I was raised here in Boston with a mother and father, but hell, they were needy too. How would he know that? I totally shut down when he straight up asked who didn't keep their promises to me. I owe him an apology. Right now, however, I think there's something else he might want from me—and I'd be lying if I said I didn't want it too.

"What was that you said about fucking like bunnies?" I ask coyly, and step away from him, backing up until I'm in the dark shadows.

"I don't think we can hold it against them. If we had a place together, we'd fuck like bunnies and drive everyone out, too."

The rooftop goes silent, his words hovering in the air as I envision the two of us cohabitating. Even though everything about it goes against what I want, a place of my own, and no commitment. Heck, I know people only want me when they want something from me. Yet, despite all that, the idea doesn't upset me. In fact, it sort of excites me.

He's not suggesting you get a place together, Melanie, so get it together.

"Hey, where did you go?" he asks playfully, nothing in his voice to suggest he wanted to cohabitate. Dammit, what is wrong with me.

"Marco..."

11

BRADY

Panting, I press my forehead to Lanie's, and stare at her pretty face beneath the moonlight. I fucked her twice today, and dammit, my dick is still inside her, snug and warm after the perfect orgasm and I already want her again.

"I've never had sex on one of these lounge chairs before," she murmurs, and I shift to keep the bulk of my weight off her.

"Glad to hear that."

"Now who's the one who sounds jealous," she teases.

I laugh. "I'm surprised we didn't break the damn thing." I slowly inch out of her, and miss her warmth as I stand. We'd haphazardly tossed our clothes everywhere when we stripped and jumped into the pool just before I ravished her. Now she crosses her arms as I reach for the pool side towel and wrap her in one, using the other to wipe between her legs. She quivers as I gently clean her up.

Once done, we both dress. Instead of leaving and locking up, she sinks back into the lounge chair, zero urgency about her even though I know she's tired. Unable to help myself, I bend and kiss her.

"Thank you," she whispers, her palm cupping my face and I lean into her touch.

As my insides quiver, fearing I might be getting in deep with this woman, I blow her off with a joke. "There you go thanking me again."

She goes quiet, contemplative, and I'm about to ask what's on her mind when she speaks.

"I owe you an apology."

"Are you kidding me? The sex was phenomenal. You don't owe me an apology for anything and I'm the one who owes you a thank you for getting naked with me."

She sits up, and I put my legs on either side of the chair and drop into it, facing her. She blinks several times and I sense a new kind of vulnerability, a nervousness about her. My throat constricts as I wait for her to elaborate.

She finally breaks the quiet, her body tensing. "No, Brady. I owe you an apology for this afternoon. You asked me a serious question, and I brushed you off. That wasn't right of me." I draw in a breath as she runs her fingers up and down my arm, the seriousness about her sending warning messages to my brain. "I just don't like to talk about my past."

"You don't have to."

"I know." She glances up, and I follow her gaze, staring at the stars twinkling overhead. "I think I might want to."

Her body begins to shake and I don't think it's from the night air. I move closer and put my hands on her legs as she crosses them. "Okay."

"You and me," she begins. "We're not so different. I used to think we were complete opposites, but not so much anymore."

"Is that why you always avoided me? You thought we were too different?"

"Yes and no." She glances past my shoulders, staring into the dark of the night. "I avoided you because I'm not looking for a relationship."

"Right, which is why we're banging and poking," I tell her quickly as she focuses back in on me. "I'm not looking for more, either," I continue, just in case she thinks I might be falling for her or something.

She nods in understanding. I told her enough for her to know I can't take on the responsibility of one more person in my life.

What if you let some of the other responsibilities go?

Knowing I can't do that, I lightly stroke her legs, heating her with my palms, and wait for her to continue. "I worked a lot." After that statement, she goes quiet and glances down, and folds her arms across her body when a hard shiver moves through her. I take a clean towel and drape it over her shoulders to keep her warm. But I don't think her chill is from the cool night air. "I made money, but my parents always took it."

Okay, that takes me by surprise. I don't think she wants pity —hell, I wouldn't want it—so I don't tell her I'm sorry. "Why did they do that?"

"Drinking, gambling...always out of work." Her eyes lift and move over my face, and I keep my expression neutral. She's not looking to shock me. "I always wanted their approval." A beat of silence and then. "I always wanted their love."

My throat tightens to the point of pain, making my next words hard to push out. "They withheld it."

Her laugh is harsh, almost maniacal. "Oh yeah." I rub my hand along her arm, offering warmth and comfort. "Here's the thing, Brady. When I tell you there's always a catch, it's because there is. People don't give without wanting something in return."

"I'm confused. They took your money, and wanted something in return?" I take in the pain on her face and as I try to wrap my brain around that, anger and sorrow, rage and hurt hit at once. I run one hand through my hair, unable to handle the bevy of emotions. Not that I'm surprised, I've always buried them.

Pain registers in her eyes. "No," she whispers that one word shattering around her as she swallows hard. "It was me. I was the one who wanted something in return."

"You?" I realize I'm still drunk on lust, but none of this is making sense. "I don't get it."

"I'm the awful one. I didn't give, without wanting in return." Pain morphs into guilt as her eyes slide away. "I was the one who wanted something, so you see, I know first-hand what tit for tat means because I was that person. I was the one who gave money, and wanted something in return."

Protectiveness grips every bone in my body. "Lanie." I touch her chin, bring her gaze back to mine. "No, baby. You are not the awful one. If your parents withheld love and you gave them all your money because you thought it would make them love you, that's on them. Kids shouldn't have to pay for their parents' love."

She takes a fueling breath, her eyes full of compassion—for me—as they search my face. "Just like kids shouldn't have to be responsible for their parents," she whispers quietly, but she's not trying to be mean. Her words are coming from her heart, and a part of me knows she's right—has always known things were backward at home. It's just...I'm responsible for them. It's the way it's been since we lost Dad.

Should it be that way, though, Brady?

"I guess none of our parents could stand on their own two feet, and counted on us in different ways." The thing is, Melanie is trying to get me to see my childhood for what it is, wanting me to let things go, but holds guilt for her own actions, unable to see it how I do.

"But mine promised they'd do things with me. Hell, all I really wanted was their attention, maybe play a board game or something. I wasn't asking for big, elaborate trips." She sniffs and wipes her nose with the towel. "They were always so happy, and full of promises before I handed the money over, then boom, they were too busy, or sick, and couldn't do any of the things they'd promised. Yet, I fell for it every damn time. You know what Einstein says." She snorts out a cynical laugh. "The definition of insanity is doing the same thing over and over and expecting a different result."

With her face tightening warily, and paling slightly, she uncrosses her knees and I stand, moving in behind her. I adjust the back of the chair, sit back down and settle her against my chest. I lightly stroke my hands through her hair, and remain quiet as she deals with her thoughts.

She exhales slowly. "Nothing but broken promises..."

At least now I understand why she doesn't expect anyone to hold up their end of the bargain, and has commitment issues. She expects everyone to drop the ball, and it does remind me that we can't have more. What if I promised her something and couldn't be there for her—like I couldn't be there for my mom when I wrapped my car around a tree.

Yeah, okay, I see that a little more clearly now, thanks to Melanie, but it doesn't change the fact that my biggest fear is for someone to need me and me letting them down. It could so easily happen and if I ever did that to a woman who's had nothing but broken promises in her life, I could never live with myself.

"I went to see a school counselor, and that's when things really changed for me."

"For the better, I'm guessing, because look at you now, Lanie. You're an amazing woman."

She gives a barely there chuckle, but it's forced. "Thanks. I'm trying to better myself."

"You *are* bettering yourself."

"That could change if I don't make this next tuition payment," she jokes, but there's an underlying truth to her words. I should know. I joke about everything to hide the truth, just like she is now. "Anyway, the counselor set me up with a psychologist."

"How did you manage to pay for that? It's not like your parents were going to help out."

"Right," she says her body stiffening, and I can almost feel the tension coiling through her. "You're pretty smart, Brady."

"Not just a pretty face and hockey player," I tease and place one hand on her stomach.

"I had to hide my money," she admits, her voice cracking slightly. A beat of silence stretches on for a few moments, that truth hovering in the air before she continues to speak. "I had to tell my parents that my shifts were cut short, or that my shift was canceled and things like that. I hated lying, you know how much I hate liars, but the only way to go was to hide the money. The psychologist was really helping me."

"I'm so happy to hear you were getting the help you needed." Although I sense this story is going to go dark, and fast.

Her muscles tighten and I can almost feel the effort it's taking to push the words past her tongue. I give her hand a squeeze, and for the first time ever Lanie feels fragile beneath my touch. "It was going so well, until my mother found my money in an old shoe box that I had hidden under my bed." A tremble goes through her and I squeeze her tight, offering her my strength and support, and her body softens as she accepts my comfort. Honestly, I never get close to women, but that's changing, right now, right here, with her, and I'm not sure I can do anything about it.

It takes effort to keep my voice steady. "She went through your stuff?"

She puts her hand over mine, like she's seeking my touch… needs it. "Yeah, they didn't believe me when I said I was losing shifts." She pauses, her breath a shallow rasp as she gives me a glimpse beneath her tough bravado. "I mean, I *was* lying to them."

I dig deep for control, when all I want to do is go find her parents and pound some sense into them. How could they not see what a treasure they had in Melanie? "You had no choice."

"I despise dishonesty, Brady. I hated it in myself at the time."

"You needed help, Lanie." I swallow against a gritty throat as my blood runs cold, rage roaring through me. My voice is deceptively calm when I say, "You did what you had to do and so maybe there's a time when dishonesty is needed."

She nods, although I sense she doesn't believe that, and continues. "I wanted the money back. I asked for it. They wouldn't give it to me and told me they needed it to pay bills, and that I was lucky I had a roof over my head. Then they told me I was to give them my next paycheck or leave."

They gave her a fucking ultimatum...

As my racing heart stutters to a stop, I note the defiant tilt of her head, and I whisper. "You left." I blow out an excruciating breath full of anger, everything in me hurting for the little girl who just wanted her parents in her life.

"I did, and it was hard, but it was the best thing that ever happened. I stayed with a friend for a bit, slept on her couch, and then her parents got tired of me so I had to quit school in my senior year, and get a job so I could find a place to live. I ended up renting a room downtown. It wasn't much, but it was mine."

I softly stroke her hair as she opens up, a new kind of vulnerability about her, one she hides from the world—and believe me, I know all about hiding. Jesus, if I didn't like her already, I sure as hell would now. I take a deep breath, an unfamiliar fullness in my chest making it a little hard to fill my lungs. I press a tender kiss to her temple. "You did the right thing."

"I never felt like I had anything that was mine before. For the first time, I never had to worry things were going to be taken from me in a moment's notice."

My heart thumps for the little lost girl who had nothing but struggles, but dammit, I admire her courage and strength to walk away from that horrible situation. Fuck, this woman deserves a family—a real family. I reach for her hand and find it trembling.

"A few years later, I ran into my psychologist and she was the one to convince me to get my GED." She tilts her head back to look at me, a deep determination on her face. "She encouraged me and after I got it, I decided I wanted more."

I squeeze her hand tighter, breathing in the fruity scent of her hair and her lightly fragranced skin. "You deserve more and you're all kinds of amazing, Lanie."

"Thank you." She wiggles, snuggling in tighter against me. "I enrolled in college years ago and now I'm doing my masters. I want to help others."

I really love that about her. "Do you see your parents? Do they have any idea just how amazing you turned out, despite them?"

"No," she tells me, her voice thinning to a whisper. "That was the end of the relationship." There's hurt in those words, but there's also healing.

We both go quiet for a long time, lost in our thoughts. After a while, I break it and say, "You know, not everyone breaks promises. Not everyone wants something for nothing." She stays quiet and I add, "I bet you're going to tell your clients that."

"Yeah," she answers quietly. "And I know what you're going to say next."

"In my head again, are you?"

She chuckles, a new lightness about her, and I can't help but think after opening up, and sharing that painful past with me has somehow lessened the weight of it. "No, I just know you're going to say, I don't know how to take my own advice. I've heard it from Brighton, too."

"Maybe I was going to say, how about you let me take you back home, and put my cock in you again?"

She sits up, turning to me, desire flickering across her face. "I like the idea of that."

Jesus, everything about this woman throws me off balance. I stand and pull her to her feet. Her body bangs against mine as my hands span her small waist and she shakes her head, a tiny laugh bubbling in her throat.

"What?" I ask.

As fatigue overtakes her, she covers her mouth and tries to stifle a yawn. "What is it about us?"

"Meaning?"

"After sex, we both spill our deepest, darkest secrets."

"Yeah, crazy," I agree, my chest tightening.

She laughs. "Damn emotions."

I stiffen at that one word. Emotions and vulnerability. Something I was never allowed to feel, something I had to constantly hide. But dammit, I can't seem to do that around this woman, can't seem to ignore the fullness in my chest. Everything in her honesty—my own honesty when I'm with her—has created a new kind of closeness, intimacy between us, and I can't let that happen. Fuck, I don't believe in love at first sight or instalove. Christ, we've only been sleeping with each other for one weekend. No one falls that fast.

Ah, but you've been watching her from afar for a long time now, dude.

"We should get back home. I have some footage I need to go over tomorrow before Noah and I have our conditioning the next day." That's when another thought hits. "Maybe I should go sleep in my own bed," I suggest, even though all I want to do is take her to bed and make sweet love to her all night long. *Sweet love? Who are you, Brady?* "We don't want our friends to catch us in bed together and get the wrong idea."

She cocks her head. "What idea would that be?"

"That we're sleeping together."

"So," she teases, drawing out that one word. "The right idea."

"Uh, yeah."

She grabs my T-shirt and tugs, the corner of her mouth lifting in a half smile. "Come on, Coddy. I already told Brighton. But don't worry, our secret is safe with her and Noah."

I follow her, my thoughts on my friends, and the things we discussed tonight at the pool. If she doesn't want anyone to know, it might be too late. I scrub my chin, worry niggling its way through my body as she glances at me over her shoulder.

She must sense the unease in me, because her eyes narrow, and her smile falters when she asks, "Did you tell Conner?"

12

MELANIE

The morning sun shines in through the windows and I roll to check the time. It's early, and I have no idea why I'm not asleep. After sex with Brady at the pool, and again here in this bed, you'd think I'd still be asleep until tomorrow morning.

I turn slowly, not wanting to wake him, and my heart jumps into my throat at the gorgeous man sprawled across the bed, taking up well over half of it. I had no idea how much I liked to snuggle until him, and honestly, it's hard to believe how much I told him last night. I don't regret it. He was an apt listener and offered comfort and support. For a guy who does nothing but joke around, he sure knows when to be quiet and thoughtful.

I should try to go back to sleep, although I know it's futile. I have a lot on my mind with school and needing to find a place to live and the second I close my eyes again, I know my brain is going to start racing. Sticking one foot out and then the other, I try to make a quiet escape. I only manage to lift myself halfway up when a big arm pins me down.

"Where do you think you're going?"

I laugh as he hauls me back down and buries his face in the side of my neck. His breath is warm on my flesh and seeps under my skin, arousing me all over again. How is that possible? I think I've had more sex this weekend than I've had my entire life. That's kind of sad, really.

"I was going to make us coffee."

He positions me under his naked body. "Coffee is overrated."

"I'm not sure I agree with that."

"Okay, how about this..." He takes one nipple into his mouth and sucks gently. "This is better than coffee."

I arc into him and sink deep into my pillow. "I really like coffee. It helps perk me up."

He chuckles against my skin and presses hot, wet kisses to my other nipple. "You seem to be perking up to me." I lift my hips as he rolls the soft blade of his tongue over my puckered nipple.

I rake my hands through his mess of hair. "Coffee warms me up."

"I'll take that challenge." He slides down my body more, his hot lips leaving a wet trail as he sinks lower and lower, until he's between my legs. He slides his hands under my backside and lifts my sex to him, moaning like I'm a buffet and he's about to eat his fill.

The first lick of his tongue against my clit sends shards of heat through me, and I reach up and grab the bed slats, shamelessly wiggling my sex against his face.

"Warm?" he murmurs from deep between my legs.

"Yes, but coffee gives me a boost of serotonin and dopamine. That puts me in a good mood."

"Ah." His grin is wicked as he slides a thick finger inside me. "How lucky that I know another way to boost your mood."

"You do?" I ask, feigning surprise. He dips his head again and treats my clit to his hot tongue as he slides his finger in and out of me until I'm practically vibrating around him. "Oh yes, I think you might be on to something."

His moans thrill me as he moves his head, his hair tickling the inside of my thighs and adding to the sweet sensations. Delicious warmth spreads over my skin as I lose myself in the things he's doing to me. I lift my pelvis, demanding more. He slides another finger inside me, and a hard quiver nearly renders me senseless.

"Like that, Lanie."

I moan, unable to find my words as my jaw goes slack, pleasure taking over every inch of my body. I take deep breaths, my pulse jackhammering in my neck as I begin to fly higher and higher.

"Brady..." He slowly drags the tips of his fingers over the hot bundle of nerves inside me, as he sucks my clit harder. My breath comes in a ragged burst as pleasure erupts between my legs. He growls with satisfaction as my sex tightens and my liquid heat coats his fingers and his mouth. Fingers still inside me, he wrings out every last inch of pleasure until I'm a hot, quivering mess beneath him.

A moment later he climbs up my body, brushing my damp hair from my forehead. There's a new kind of calmness about him. Yes, the hard erection pressing against me lets me know he needs to be inside me, but he's not rushing, not overly eager, like it might be our last time.

No, this time he's sliding into me slowly, offering me one sweet inch at a time. Matching his mood, I reach around him and lightly run my fingers up and down his back. His lips capture mine, and the kiss is slow, tender, leisurely, but no less passionate than before. I moan as I taste my sweetness on his lips.

He breaks the soft kiss and lightly runs his tongue over my bottom lip. Our eyes meet and hold, and the intimacy I spot there, the bevy of emotions he's not blinking away, curls around my shuddering heart. What is happening between us? Or is it just me?

His heart pounds against my chest as he fills me with his cock. Eyes half closed, he moans my name, and as I moan his, something warm and foreign rushes to my heart. I bring his mouth back to mine, overwhelmed at what I'm feeling, and not wanting him to see it—identify it.

I lift my hips, welcoming each glorious thrust. "So good."

"Babe, Jesus," he murmurs into my mouth, those two words broken, slightly fractured. God, is something going on inside him too? I begin to tremble from head to toe, tension building inside both of us as he thickens even more. I whimper, and even though I'm wrung out from that last climax, his cock is coaxing another one from me.

I move against him, grind my clit into his pelvis and the world shuts down around me as I give into the pleasure.

"Fuck, Lanie." He takes a gulping breath as my sex muscles squeeze his cock, and he drives in deep, giving me every inch of him to clench around. He peppers my mouth with kisses as I ride out the waves.

He grunts, my liquid heat searing his cock, and from the way he's clenching down on his jaw, it's clear he's struggling, wanting to hold on until I finish. I put my mouth near his ear.

"Fill me with your cum, Coddy."

"Christ, woman." He grips my hips for leverage, pulls out, and slides back in again. I moan as he fills me, loving the way his cock is pulsing, seconds from climax. He buries his face in my neck, his hot panting breaths warming my flesh. A low, guttural sound crawls out of his throat as he lets go, and fills me with his seed. His head lifts and I silence his growls with a kiss.

Our lips linger and we stay sealed as one, our bodies cooling as he grows flaccid. He pulls out of me, and winces, which pulls a chuckle from me. He rolls off me to stand. "Be right back."

He comes back with a washcloth and my heart misses a beat. Without words, he sits beside me and cleans me up, then disappears again. This time he's gone for a good long time, and I sit up, listening for sounds. Did he leave? I'm about to get up and dress and find out what's going on when he comes back into the room, two cups of coffee in hand.

"Thank you." He hands me one and I take a sip.

He cocks his head, completely comfortable standing beside the bed stark naked. "What do you think?

I give a cat-like stretch, my sigh of pleasure filling the room. "I like what I see."

He laughs. "No, about the coffee. Overrated?"

I take another sip and moan as I set it on the nightstand. I crook my finger and he drops down next to me. I put my arms around him and pull his mouth to mine. Our kiss is soft and tender, much like our lovemaking was.

Lovemaking?

Good God, he really did mess with my serotonin and dopamine levels if I'm calling what we did lovemaking. It was just sex and I can't forget that.

"If I could wake up like that every day, I'd probably never drink another cup again."

A car horn honks in the parking lot, and he sits up a bit straighter. "I supposed I should get out of here before Noah and Brighton get back."

"It's still early, but yeah, I should get up, clean this place, and bus back to my place."

"You're taking the bus?"

"Car. Broken. Remember?" I pick up the coffee again and take a drink. Mmm, hazelnut. "If I'm not careful, I could get addicted."

He puts his hand on my bare leg and runs it up and down. "Are you talking about the coffee, or my cock?"

I glance down and, as if hearing the call, his cock jumps. "Maybe both."

He leans in and kisses me, lingering for an extra moment before saying, "I'll drive you."

"You don't have to do that."

He stands, and I take in his most perfect ass as he goes searching for his clothes. "Where's your car?"

"It's in the driveway back at my place in the city. It wouldn't start and I didn't have the funds to call a tow truck. Last night's tips helped, though. Your friends are good tippers."

He glances at me over one broad shoulder, his brow cocked, a fierceness about him. "They better tip you well or they'll have me to deal with."

"Ooh, my protective hero."

He winks at me. "Want to grab breakfast on the way?"

"You really don't have to drive me and I can whip up something here. I make a mean waffle, and I don't know if you noticed, but there's like three cans of whipped cream in the fridge." I don't want him spending money on me, and I brought groceries when I came. Brighton told me not to, but I like to pay my own way.

"Okay, sounds good." He glances at my cup. "More coffee?"

"Yes, please."

"Why don't you run and shower and I'll drop a pod in the machine."

"Not joining me?"

"Do you want to get out of here today or not?" he teases.

I tap my chin, like I'm debating that, but I do have a lot to do today, and I want to go over those apartments he saved for me to look at. I'm going to have to make some phone calls.

"Fine." I jump from the bed. "Did any of those apartments you searched have open houses today?"

"Yeah, a couple. You want to go look?"

"I might do that later."

"I can take you."

"Aren't you just Mr. Helpful today." Of course, he doesn't need to waste his day driving me around to see places. "I'm sure you have better things to do."

Conflicting emotions flicker in his eyes before he gives a casual shrug and flashes me a grin. "I was going to go over some video footage of our games, but I have a thing for damsels in distress."

I laugh at that, and throw a pillow at him. "I'm anything but, and thank you, but I can do it alone." I do like how he takes his job seriously, even spending weekends going over old games to learn from them. Does that sound like something a jokester does—a guy who wants everyone to think he's nothing but a bucking good time? As I think about that, I search the floor for my clothes.

"Okay." I hear a crack in that one word and lift my head to see him. The second my gaze lands on his, he plasters on a smile, and it's easy to tell it's forced. Dammit, did I hurt his feelings? He steps up to me, playful demeanor back in place, and whacks my ass. "Go, shower." I yelp and dart into the hall. I leave the bathroom door cracked, just in case, and my body is gloriously warm, my brain buzzing with happiness as I turn the water on and climb into the shower. I begin humming and when I catch myself, I laugh. When did I ever hum in the shower?

When was I ever so happy?

I wash quickly, rinse, and step from the shower to find Brady standing right there with a big towel, a hot cup of coffee and an appreciative smile. It's that smile as he looks at me that makes me feel like I'm the most important woman in the world to him, even though I'm not. I take the towel and wrap myself in it, and accept the mug. A girl could get used to this. I don't tell him that. No need to scare him off. "Your turn. I'll get dressed and get to work on breakfast."

He slaps my ass and I yelp as I walk past. Back in the bedroom, I pull on a pair of shorts and a T-shirt, and make my way to the living room to pack my books into my backpack. I glance around the big space, hoping someday, when I have a good job and a good paycheck, I can have a place like this to myself. God, why does that thought suddenly feel empty in the pit of my stomach? Spending one glorious weekend with Brady does not change what I want, or how I have always envisioned my future.

I need to get out of this place.

I set my bags by the door and walk to the kitchen, glancing out the window and smiling as guests play in the surf. When I do get a full-time job, I am going to miss this place, and the pool parties at the rooftop bar. Then again, I can always visit. I've become pretty close to Brighton, and I know she'll extend an invite.

I pull the eggs from the fridge and the other ingredients needed from the pantry, as the image of me attending with Brady's arm around me hits like a brick to the face. Whoa, I can't be thinking like that. But I know how I should be thinking. Brady didn't have much of a childhood, always taking care of others, and I know quite a bit about that, so for the next couple of weeks, I simply want us to have some fun and make up for those lost years.

I spot my laptop on the counter, and open it to find a message from Brady with the apartment listings. I scan them and find myself humming again as the shower rains down on Brady and I pull the waffle maker from the cupboard and mix up the batter. I clean some berries and grab a can of whipped cream, and, after deciding Brady and I needed to reclaim our lost childhood, spray it straight into my mouth.

Brady comes around the corner. "Hey, share."

I hold the can up. He has different ideas. He slides an arm around my waist, and pulls me to him, the way I've grown accustomed to and yeah, I really love it. My body bumps his, and I breathe in his warm soapy scent as his lips fall over mine. He moans, and it sends a jolt of need through me.

"Baby, you taste good." He inches back, wipes his finger over my bottom lip and puts it into his mouth. "Yum." He holds me tighter. "Now I want to taste you all over again."

"While I'd like that—"

"No, I get it. You have things to do, and apartments to check out."

I run my finger over the tip of the cannister, and put my finger into his mouth. His eyes are full of heat and curiosity as he licks it clean. "But that doesn't mean I don't want a rain check."

"Anytime."

I pick up the spatula and give his backside a whack. "Now, go sit while I cook breakfast." He laughs and goes for the coffee. "What time is your conditioning tomorrow?" I ask.

"Afternoon. Few hours. Why? You want to watch? Can't get enough of Coddy?"

I laugh at his playfulness. "No. Just curious."

"Do you work tomorrow?" he asks, his voice less jovial.

"Eleven to six."

"That doesn't leave much time for studying."

I mix the batter until there are no lumps. I have no idea why Brighton and Noah's daughter Camryn always asks for lumps in her pancakes. Strange child.

"No," I respond and cast him a fast glance. "But I think we did pretty well on chapter four."

He wags his eyebrows. "I love chapter four." I laugh at his antics. "Your final exam is when?"

"Two weeks from last Friday. Then I have a week off before the next semester starts. I don't normally do summer semesters, but I really wanted this professor."

"All work and no play."

I point my spatulas at him. "Makes Melanie a great counselor."

"Yeah, it does." I realize the man knows all about hard work. He wouldn't be where he is without it. Instead of sitting, he steps up behind me, pulls my hair to the side and places a tender kiss on the sensitive spot he discovered last night. A fine quiver goes through me. "How many more courses do you have before you finish?"

"One this fall, and one in the winter semester, then I'm done."

"We'll have a big celebration after you finish your exam."

Celebration? The last time I celebrated something was...well, I don't think I've ever celebrated anything in my entire life. "No, we don't have to do that." I don't believe in being frivolous about anything.

"I want to."

Little alarm bells jangle like they always do when someone tells me they want to do something for me. Probably because I'm used to them wanting something in return. "Why?"

"Simply because I want to. How is that for a reason?"

I frown into the batter. "There's always a reason."

"Hey." He puts his arms around my waist and hugs me. "Can't a guy just want to do something for no other reason than he wants to? Maybe it makes me happy just to see you happy."

I sway against his body. "I'm not convinced," I tell him, a garbled laugh catching in my throat.

"Let me convince you."

The idea of celebrating does sound kind of fun. "Brady—"

He growls into my ear as he nips at me. "Leave it with me."

"I don't want a party or anything big," I warn.

"No party, or anything big, got it." I shake my head and pour the batter into the waffle maker. He moans as the batter begins to bubble. "Dammit, that smells good."

"Are you talking about me or the waffles?" I tease, realizing he's changing the subject.

"Maybe both." He chuckles against my neck just as his phone rings. His mood instantly changes, and he backs up. I steal a quick glance at him as he pulls his phone from his pocket.

"I have to take this."

I nod, and get to work on finishing our breakfast. His mood is somber when he comes back and I can only guess it was a family member looking for something from him.

"These look delicious," he says and I don't press, sensing he doesn't want to talk about it. I turn the conversation to the apartments for rent, and we talk about that as we eat. Once done, we clear the dishes together, and I begin to clean up all evidence of my presence this weekend. I want the place spotless for Brighton when she gets back.

"I'm all set," I tell Brady when I'm done cleaning and putting new sheets on the bed.

We start toward the door, but before we reach it, it bursts open. The second little Camryn sees us both standing there, she throws her arms out. "Uncle Brady!" she yells at the top of her lungs and darts to him.

"Indoor voice, Camryn," Brighton corrects as she rubs her belly.

I grin and still my steps as Noah comes in with the bags. "Hey, you two are back early." Behind them, Mabel, their big Bernese Mountain dog comes barreling in and she too goes straight for Brady. He does have a way with women. He drops down, setting Camryn on his knee, and pats Mabel like she's his best friend in the world. It's so goddamn adorable and sweet, the whipped cream pales in comparison.

"Hey, Mel." Luggage in hand, Noah walks down the hall and sets the bags by the dryer.

"Hey, Noah."

"Camryn has a birthday party to go to," Brighton explains. "She was anxious to get back and get herself all prettied up. I think there's a boy she likes."

"Last I heard, she didn't want anything to do with boys."

Brighton arches a playful brow, because yeah, I get it. Last she heard, I didn't want to have anything to do with boys either. As I shake my head at her, she glances at my bags by the door. "You know you don't have to leave. We have plenty of vacant rooms on the lower level."

"Staying here for the weekend was just what I needed, and I'm not going to take advantage of your generosity. Besides, Brady found some places online that might be suitable and I'm sure the bang fest back home is over by now."

She leans in conspiratorially. "Speaking of bang fest." Brady's head lifts, and heat colors my cheeks when a grin toys with the corner of his mouth.

"Brighton," I warn under my breath.

"Oops," she chuckles when she realizes he heard too. She blinks innocently, which isn't so innocent at all. "Sometimes I too forget to use my indoor voice."

Ohmigod, I'm going to kill her.

13

___

BRADY

___

Seagulls squawk loudly as we step outside. We walk to my car and I hit the fob to let Melanie in as I drop her bags into the back seat. She slides into the passenger seat, and I walk around the car. It would be so much easier for her if she just accepted Brighton's offer to stay in one of the spare rooms. It's not in her nature, and there's a big part of me that admires a woman who doesn't want to take advantage of others.

But what she doesn't realize is that it's okay to accept help from friends. No part of me thinks she'd ever take advantage of anyone. As that thought jumps around inside my brain, my thoughts go back to my morning conversation with my uncle. Apparently, he needs a new SUV—to help drive my mother to her appointments. The picture of the vehicle he sent is pretty fucking fancy if you ask me.

When I actually questioned him on it, he went on to let me know how lucky I was that I was in Boston while he was taking care of my mother. When I asked where Mom was, and if I could speak to her, it eventually came out that she went to St. George Street in St. Johns with my cousin—the same cousin I sent money to for skates—to do some shopping.

Jesus, I never used to question any of this before. I just knew —because it was what I was always led to believe—that it was my responsibility to take care of them.

Is it your responsibility, Brady?

"Everything okay?" Melanie asks as I climb into the driver's seat.

"My uncle Wayne called. He's mom's brother. Wants money for a new SUV," I tell her, as a little burst of anger swirls around my chest. Jesus, maybe I was never allowed to exhibit emotions because they would lead me to questioning things. "I bought him a new car a couple of years ago. I guess it's not enough now."

"Does he work?" she asks and I don't miss the curious concern in her voice.

"He used to, until I signed with Boston." She nods and glances out the window. "What?" I don't give her a chance to speak, but instead, I defend my mother, like I'm used to doing and say, "He needed to be there for my mother after I left." Her hand snakes across the seat and settles on my lap. I close mine over hers and give it a squeeze. My other hand goes to my face, and I scrub my chin. "He said Mom was out shopping with my cousin." If there's no extra cash for frivolous things, why did they drive all the way to George St, in St. Johns? That's where all the bars and pubs and restaurants are. It's a popular spot for college kids. I'm pretty sure they're not shopping for school supplies there.

"Is this the cousin...the one needing the skates?"

"Yeah, I sent money right away. I said I would, so I did." I don't know why I sound defensive. "I assumed she'd already gotten them as Mom said she was desperate. Guess they must be shopping for other things."

"Is she married?" I nod. "Does her husband work?"

"Married yes, but Carl is out of work."

"That's too bad. Sounds like times are tough. What did he used to do?"

I snort. "I don't know if he ever worked."

"What about the processing plant? Sounds like it's a big place that hires a lot of people."

"Yeah," is all I say and start the car.

"Maybe he should check there. I mean, if he's fit and able." A beat and then, "Is your uncle fit and able?"

"As far as I know." Truthfully, the fishing industry might not be what it used to be, but work can be found, and people can move.

"Your mom. Did she grow up in Paradise?"

I eye her as she digs into my past, and while I'd normally shut down this kind of probing, I answer, "No, actually. She came to Newfoundland from a farming village in Ireland. They traveled here, and she met Dad and the rest was history. I think she was looking for a better life." I snort out a laugh. "I think she thought there was gold in them Grand Banks."

"I guess she didn't find what she was looking for, huh?"

"Guess not." I pull into traffic. "I think she might have resented the life, now that I think about it. Then Dad died..."

"And she pinned all her hopes on you."

Heart jumping in my chest at those harsh words, my gaze jerks to hers, and her eyes go wide as her jaw drops. She squeezes my leg. "I'm sorry, Brady. That wasn't my place to say that."

I nod, not knowing any other way to respond. I'm not mad at her... Wait, am I mad? Shit, I don't know what I'm feeling. Dealing with emotions is fucking hard and confusing. Maybe it's best just to swallow that shit down again.

"Which apartments did you decide you wanted to check out?" I ask, changing the subject. "Did you look over the links I sent you?" I realize she doesn't want me coming, and I should be happy about that. I've been saying from the very beginning that I can't take on the responsibility of one more person in my life, or one more thing, but I'd actually like to help her look.

I cast her a fast glance and she pulls her laptop from her bag. "I scanned them quickly." She opens the links and looks them over. "Do you know much about rentals, and things like that?"

"Not a whole lot. I shared a place with Theo and now I'm renting from Noah." What must she think of a grown man with a killer career still renting? Shit, I'm starting to wonder about him too.

"If you're really not too busy, I would like it if you came with me. Maybe between the two of us, we can figure out the rental market and make sure I'm paying fair price."

"Yeah, sounds good."

"As long as apartment hunting isn't keeping you from anything."

I wink at her. "It's actually keeping me from cashing that rain check and ravishing you."

"You hang on to that." She glances out the window. "Darn... looks like sunshine for the rest of the day."

I snort out a laugh. "Okay, Lanie, how do I get to your place?"

She sits back and gives me great directions and about thirty minutes later, I pull up in front of a duplex. "My roommate and I share that side." She points to the blue sedan in the driveway. I recognize the vehicle from around the resort. "That's my car having a nice long siesta in the driveway. You can pull in behind it."

"You have no idea what's wrong with it?"

"Oh, I do." She reaches for the door handle. "The engine doesn't work."

"Funny girl. Where are your keys? I'll take a look."

She eyes me. "Are you serious? You know things about vehicles?"

I shrug. "I worked on a boat, and had to do repairs. If I don't know, my buddy Ash will."

"Ash, from the team? Cute defenseman."

"Wow, you seem to know a lot about Ash."

She laughs, as I portray jealousy on purpose, of course. "Yeah, I know he's on your team and a defenseman."

"Cute. Don't forget you called him cute."

"Right, cute. I know so much, I could do his memoir."

I growl as I reach for her. "I had no idea you were such a

smart ass." I grab her arm and pull her toward me, needing a kiss before she leaves the car.

She kisses me back. "Um, I think you kind of did know that."

"Yeah, that's true."

"I always knew you were one." Her eyes bore into me, and I can almost feel her poking around inside my head. Maybe I should just go. She already knows too much about me.

"Yeah, that's right. Smart ass. That's what I am." I turn from her gaze and glance at her front door as fight or flight instincts kick in. I really should just go. This woman is far too astute for me.

"Don't ask Ash." She frowns. "I can take care of my own things. I don't want to be dragging any of your teammates into my life or problems. Come on." She opens her door, not really giving me a choice. "Let's go over the listings and see what we can view today."

"Sure." I kill the ignition and step from the car. After I grab her bags, I follow her up the walkway and stop to take a better look at her car. She opens the door and I hurry to catch up, but the second we enter the house, and hear loud sex noises coming from one of the upstairs rooms, I cringe.

"What the fuck." I drop her bags in the entranceway.

She shakes her head, her cheeks heating with embarrass-ment. "I'm so sorry. I thought they'd be chafed raw by now."

That makes me laugh. "Honestly, Lanie. I can see why you fled. They sound like two cats in an alley fight."

"Ohmigod," she giggles. "Do you think that's what we sound like?"

"Yeah, probably, but no one was listening."

She shrugs, and coming to their defense says, "They don't know we're here."

Something tells me they heard us coming and started with these antics. "They drove you out of the house Friday. They knew you were home then." It's just fucking disrespectful, and I'm beginning to think they're doing it on purpose. Her roommate wants her gone, likely so she can move her guy in. Can this woman not get a fucking break?

"Jess, I'm home, and I have company," Melanie calls out loudly. A brief moment of silence, and then an upstairs door slams shut.

"Wow." I drive my hands into my pockets. "That's fucking rude."

"I'm sorry." She lightly touches my arm and winces. "I can understand if you want to leave."

"Yeah, I fucking want to leave." She nods in understanding, as I pull one hand from my pocket and capture her hand. "And you're coming with me."

Her head rears back. "What are you talking about? I can't leave."

"Yeah, you can. Brighton offered you a room. I heard her." She glances down, staring at the pale, cracked tile on the floor, conflicting emotions moving over her beautiful yet distraught face. "Fine, if you don't want one of the downstairs rooms, you can stay with me."

Her gaze jerks back to mine. "In your suite? No, I can't do that." She shakes her head adamantly and tries to step back but I keep her hand in mine and step with her, keeping our bodies close even though her rejection feels like a hard slap to the face.

I keep my composure. "Why not?"

She blinks rapidly. "I...I..." She can't find her words, because she can't come up with a reasonable answer.

"Look, it won't be for long. We're going to look at places today, and maybe you'll find something fast, but until then, you're with me."

Her long hair falls over her shoulder as she shakes her head again. "I...I just don't want to be a bother. If I become—"

"I never said you'd be a bother." She swallows as the walls practically vibrate from the sex screams reverberating down the stairs. "Obviously, you can't stay here." Her eyes narrow, looking almost vacant, like she's remembering something unpleasant. A second later, she squares her shoulders and her lips part, no doubt about to protest. "Get your stuff. I'm not taking no for an answer." I shake my head, warning her not to fight me on this, and when a loud bang and scream that sounds more like pain than pleasure reaches our ears—did someone's head hit the fucking roof?—I can almost feel her softening.

Wanting to sweeten the deal, I remind her, "Think about how much more time you'll have to study before your big test. No transport time back and forth to the resort."

Wow, way to spin it, dude.

Hit her where you know it's going to do the most damage. The fact that I'm pushing my help on her doesn't go unnoticed. What was it that I always said about not taking on more responsibility, and here I am doing just that. Maybe I'm just used to people wanting things from me, and it's in my nature to give, or maybe I'm pushing because it's Lanie.

When she remains quiet—because that's a sweet offer too good to pass up—I continue. "I'll give you all the time you need to study, and will only ravish you at night," I tease. "Now, go pack what you need."

She gives a curt nod, the vacant look clearing from her eyes as her back goes rigid. "Right."

I give a nod in return. "It's settled then."

She holds one hand out, palm toward me. "Just promise if I get in the way—"

"You won't." I hold my hands out. "Give me your keys. I want to take a look at your car." Once again, her mouth opens and I shake my head. "Lanie," I warn.

"Fine," she blurts out and plucks a set of keys from a bowl on a table near the door. "I'll be fast."

I wince, my shoulders almost touching my ears as the screams continue. Theo was loud and obnoxious, but this takes it to a whole new level. "I'd say that's a good idea, otherwise that ridiculousness is going to drive you straight to therapy." I pull her to me, and kiss her lightly. "I'll be outside."

I wait for a second as she picks up her bags and darts up the stairs. Once she disappears from my sight, I step outside, enjoying the quiet. Not that it's all that quiet. Kids are playing in the streets, and a couple of houses down, a man is mowing his lawn. The sounds are still quieter outside.

My phone pings, and I tug it from my pocket and slide my finger across the screen. "What's up, Gunther?"

"Bunch of us are headed to Duke's for a game of pool this afternoon. Join us. I owe you a beer."

"You don't owe me a beer."

"Fuck yeah, I do. So does Conner. Come play pool and we'll pay our debt."

I wince as I glance back at the house. The guys think they owe me a beer because I stupidly bet that I could get Melanie into bed. Obviously, the bet was bogus and I didn't really think it meant anything until they asked about it on the rooftop the other night. "I can't. I uh...I'm tied up."

He laughs. "If you're blowing us off, it better be because you're *tied* to a damn bed post."

"Fuck off."

I hear a car door slam in the background, and a motor rev. "How about we go double or nothing?"

I scratch my head and glance over my shoulder to make sure Melanie isn't listening. "What are you talking about?"

"I bet you can't get her to fall in love with you. Fucking is one thing, falling for your sorry cod ass is another."

"You're saying she'd never fall for me?" My stomach tightens, because maybe that's what I really want.

"Oh, it's on, buddy."

Before I can tell him it's not, a loud laugh reverberates through the phone before he ends the call. I shake my head and walk to the car. I glance back at the house and that's when I see movement at the window. I stare for a second. Is Melanie watching me? I hope to fuck she didn't overhear anything. But no, not Melanie, it's some dude and it looks to me like he's fully dressed. Son of a bitch.

That guy and Melanie's roommate were fucking around—but not fucking at all. Bastards. Every protective instinct I possess grips me hard, and all I want to do is take Melanie home and make life a little bit fucking easier for her.

I'm about to turn when the guy's eyes go wide, and he starts to open the window. Clearly, he recognizes me.

"Hey," he calls out, wanting my attention. Without looking up, I give it to him, by means of a middle finger.

A loud laugh crawls out of my throat as I turn in the passenger seat to admire Brady's strong profile. I can't seem to pull myself together, and maybe it has more to do with the lightness inside of me, than Brady telling my roommate's boyfriend to fuck off with a hand gesture. It really was kind of funny.

I didn't even know what was happening until I heard Jess's fiancé cursing and ran to the window to see what was going on. I found Brady giving him the finger, while putting his phone to his ear. I have no idea who he called, and he didn't offer up the information. Not that it's any of my business. We're just friends with benefits for the next couple of weeks, and well, maybe more now that I'm going to be staying with him.

I take the band off my wrist and tie my hair up, still chuckling. "I can't believe you gave him the middle finger."

"He deserved it," Brady snorts as he drives through Boston's

Sunday traffic. I laugh again and he grins at me. "They're both assholes. Sorry, I know Jess is your roommate..."

"I know. But still..." I sink back into the seat. "You should have heard him curse you out."

"I did. He opened his window, remember?" He casts me a fast glance. "Did he really think I was going to be his buddy or give him an autograph after that ridiculous display of fake fucking? Screw him."

"Yeah, screw him." I chuckle as he flicks on his signal. "How about right here?"

I look to the left and see a quaint coffee shop, one I'd seen but had never been in before. "As good as any." He circles the downtown core, searching for a parking spot, but it's Sunday and busy.

"Damn tourists. Hogging all the good parking spots. Arseholes."

There's a twang in his voice when he says arseholes, and I assume it's a popular Newfoundland word. "Arseholes? Really?" I stare at him. "Aren't you a tourist yourself?"

"No, I live here. Remember?" He arches a brow and playfully does a weird bobble head thing that suggests I might have been dropped on my head at birth. The verdict is still out on that.

"Have you seen any of Boston, though?" Honestly, touring the city with him would be fun. Letting him see it through my eyes, and going on rides...well, maybe that would give him back a piece of his childhood.

He slows as a SUV pulls out of a space. "I've seen the inside of the Bucks arena. What else is there?"

"Ohmigod, Brady. Boston is full of history, shops, museums and great restaurants. You have to take in some of the downtown sights."

Once again, he casts me a joking look that suggests I might be insane. "Do I now?" Once the SUV leaves, he eases into the spot, and kills the ignition. "Come on. I have a headache from all the screaming and need a strong coffee."

Snatching up my backpack, I step from the car and on the sidewalk, we head toward the crosswalk. I note the way a few people stare, their eyes lighting as they recognize Brady. He keeps his head tucked, which is odd for a guy who supposedly loves all the limelight and attention. Oh Brady Fisher, there is so much more to you than you want the world to see. Strong fingers close around mine and hold tight, and my chest tightens around my heart as he pulls me to him, like right now, he wants the world to consist of only him and me.

We reach the coffee shop, and delicious scents fill my nostrils as he pulls the door open and puts his hand on the small of my back to usher me in. "You want to grab a table for us?"

I nod and search for a table in the busy café. As I drop into a seat and pull my laptop from my backpack, and as a loud shriek fills the space, two thoughts hit at once. Either my roommate is here and she and her partner are faking sex again, or the place is getting robbed. I stiffen as I lift my head, only to relax—slightly—when I find a group of girls surrounding Brady.

An instant wave of jealousy grips me by the throat as they throw themselves at him. Jeez, are they even fourteen? Okay fine, they're all in their early twenties and seeing the way they're dressed, with their boobs hanging out, reminds me I'm approaching thirty, and Brady is younger than me. Why the heck is he with me when he can have any of those girls, probably all at the same time?

I try to ignore all the fangirling, but it's impossible, considering more and more girls, as well as women and men, are jumping from their seats to get Brady's autograph. One of the blondes scribbles something on a napkin and stuffs it into the front of his jeans. Brady grins and smiles and when he says something to her, she laughs like it's the funniest thing she's ever heard in her life.

He's playing, joking, acting his 'usual' self—supposedly—as everything inside me twists, because I can see below the surface, see another side of him. Why does he feel like he needs to act this way? I guess maybe fans expect that of him and he's just giving them what they want. And they do want it, because they're eating up his every damn word.

"Did I see you come in with Brady Fisher?"

I turn at the voice and find an elderly lady at the table beside me, leaning toward me. "Oh, yes. Are you a fan?"

"My grandson is. Do you think he'd give me an autograph?"

"I'm sure he would. I can ask him when he gets back to the table."

"I can't compete with those young girls." She chuckles, and once again unease hits because I can't compete either. Why again is Brady with me? "They'd probably trample me if I tried to get close."

"You stay seated. He'll give you an autograph when he comes back."

"You're sweet dear. Are you related to Brady? An older sister perhaps?"

Really? My stomach squeezes tight. I know I'm not fourteen like those girls, but do I really look like I could be his older sister? Is it out of the realm that I could be his girlfriend? I mean I'm not, but is it really so far-fetched? Heck, maybe it is.

I plaster on my best smile. "We're friends."

I steal a glance at Brady as he lets out a big laugh, and I work to fight down the pang of jealousy—not to mention the fact that this woman thought I was his older sister—as I boot up my laptop. I do my very best to check out the listings, and I send off a couple of emails for afternoon viewings. Though I'm sure we'll make them, not if Brady is going to continue entertaining fans all afternoon.

God, Melanie, get it together.

Ten minutes pass, and he finally shows up at the table, two mugs of coffee in hand. "Sorry about that." He sets the coffee down and slides one my way.

I try for casual and wave a dismissive hand. "No worries. You have fans, I get it." I gesture with a nod toward the elderly lady blinking eagerly as she waits for his attention. "This lovely lady would like an autograph for her grandson."

"Oh sure." He turns his attention to the lady, talks to her for a minute and signs a sheet of paper she pulled from her purse. Two big steps and he's back at our table. "Any good leads?" he asks.

"I guess I could you the same thing." I wince as soon as the words leave my mouth. "Sorry. I think I'm just still upset from the way Jess and her boyfriend were acting." It's as good an excuse for my behavior as any, but I'm not sure he's buying it. Dammit, I don't want him to think I'm jealous. If he knew

I 'might be' catching feelings, he wouldn't be so quick to offer me a place to stay. I mean at first, I was wondering why he would, until he talked about ravishing me. Tit for tat. Jeez, it almost sounds like I'm pimping myself out for a place to stay. I'm not, because I actually want to be with him again.

His dark eyes hold sympathy as they move over my face. "I guess it's not easy realizing you're where you're not wanted, eh?"

"She could have asked me to move out."

His hand snakes across the table and closes over mine, giving it a squeeze. "I'm sorry."

Wanting to lighten things I say. "No worries, eh."

He laughs. "Nice Canadian slang. Almost mistook you for a Newfoundlander." He takes a sip of coffee as I reach for mine. "Hey, wait, you still haven't kissed the cod."

I choke as I swallow. "Um, yeah." He laughs and if I'm not mistaken, his cheeks have turned a shade of pink.

"Right. Okay." He shifts, pulling his hand from mine to adjust his pants. "Let's talk about something else, shall we?" The server comes over, and sets two cinnamon rolls in front of us, and she gives Brady a big smile.

"See you soon."

My heart stalls, and I do my best not to show any kind of reaction as she ignores me like the bitch she is, and goes back behind the counter. I focus hard on my screen and Brady explains. "She has season tickets." I nod, and he takes my hand again. "I told you. You and me, until the pre-season."

Heat goes through me, and my heart stumbles a bit, and dammit that is not supposed to happen. I pull my hand away and pick up the cinnamon roll. I'm not even hungry after breakfast, but this looks delicious. I bite into it and moan as sugar and spice and cinnamon burst on my tongue.

"Ohmigod, Brady, this is delicious."

"Yeah, well." He shifts uncomfortably, adjusting his pants. "If you keep moaning like that, I'm going to take you back to your place, because it's closer than mine, and give your room-mate a run for her money."

I laugh and it almost hurts to swallow. I take a sip of coffee to help me push the roll down, and Brady takes his chair and moves it to sit beside me.

"Focus, Lanie. Focus," he jokes as he turns the laptop so he can see the screen. "Okay, this is the one I thought you'd really like."

I scrunch up my nose as I take in the price. "If I didn't have a full year of school left, this might be more doable. I have to save for tuition and don't really have savings to dip in to." I really hate discussing money with anyone, but if he's helping me search, I need to be honest about my finances.

"I'd better get my guys to start upping their tips."

"No, they're great as it is. Let's just find something else."

He nods and we scroll and search until we come across a place that isn't too far out of my budget. "Hey, this looks good. I could manage it if I eat more boxed macaroni and cheese."

"You like that one?"

Of all the ones available, this is really the only one that's suit-able. "Not bad. One bedroom, kitchen is small, but that's okay, and it's right near the T."

"Once you get your car fixed, you won't need to take the subway."

"True," I agree, as he pulls his phone from his pocket. He punches in a number, and I frown. Who is he calling? The second he starts talking, I realize he's calling the apartment to see if we can view it. He nods as the woman on the other end speaks and I take another bite of my cinnamon roll. This time I don't moan, and he can thank me for that later.

He ends the call, and checks the time. "We can view it right now. Only problem is, it's a sublet, and won't be available until November."

I turn my attention back to the laptop. "I guess we'd better keep looking."

He reaches across the small café table and picks up his cinnamon roll. "November isn't that far away."

"It's far enough. I can't stay with you that long."

"Really, Lanie, I won't even be home that much. Not with practice and the season starting. You'll pretty much have the place to yourself. Occupancy rates are down all over town, and if this is the apartment that suits you, you'd be smart to stay with me until it's available." He bites into his cinnamon roll. "Holy shit, this is the best thing I've ever put in my mouth."

I grin. "Right."

He washes down the roll with a big drink of coffee. "Right as in you think it's smart to stay with me, or right as in this is the best thing I've ever put in my mouth."

"The second thing." I know he's trying to help me out, but I've come to learn the man has enough people counting on him. He's always giving, and getting nothing in return. Except this time he's getting sex and while that's good for both of us, maybe there are things I can do to make his life easier.

He touches my hair and twirls it around his finger. "What's going on inside that big brain of yours?"

"Maybe the first thing too." The smile that crosses his face, like he's genuinely happy that I'm agreeing to stay with him, messes with my 'big brain' a little—makes me consider that there could be more than just sex going on between us.

Don't go there, girl. Lessons learned taught you that love comes with a price.

"Then let's go view this place." He takes a big drink of his coffee and sets it down. "I'm taking this with me, though." He picks up the cinnamon roll and I grab mine.

"Me too."

As we head toward the doors, all eyes once again turn to us and I listen to the hushed murmurs. Brady grabs my hand, but quickly lets it go when another group of girls come in through the door. For a second, I'm taken aback by the abruptness of it all, until he reaches into his pocket and pulls out the napkin that blonde girl stuffed in there earlier. He drops it into the trash can and I can't help but grin.

I like that.

I like him.

Damn.

15

BRADY

"How the hell did I let you talk me into this." I tug my hat lower on my head as I shake it, feigning annoyance.

Melanie arches a brow. "Don't tell me you're not having fun?"

As I sit on the top level of the iconic orange and green double decker tour bus, I fold my arms and stare at the downtown sights as the commentator gives information about Boston's most popular attractions. "Fine, I won't."

"You loved the Boston Tea Party Ship and Museum. I saw you grinning when you didn't know I was watching."

"Grinning? I wasn't grinning. I was cringing because I had an itch on my back that I couldn't scratch." I'm teasing her, and she knows it. I've been having a great day getting on and off the Trolly at different locations and actually getting to know the city I live in for the first time, and yes, I was like a kid in a candy store when we walked Griffin's wharf and enjoyed the protest's reenactment. Today is actually a nice break from all the training I've been doing with the team, and Melanie has been studying hard, and needed the break too.

She takes my hand and gives it a squeeze and I give her a teasing smile. She's been staying with me for the past week, and what a hell of a week it's been. A guy could get used to having a girl like her around, and while I've gotten used to going home to an empty place, I have to say, I've been looking forward to our evenings together. Sure, the sex is great, but so is the friendship, and I love sitting down and watching a movie together before bed.

I turn my attention back to the sights when my phone pings, and I reach for it, somehow expecting it to be my family back home. I'd just deposited a chunk of change into Mom's account, but that doesn't mean she's not looking for me. I'm pleasantly surprised when I see it's a message from my buddy Ash. I called him from Melanie's place the day I convinced her to pack her things and come live with me, and asked him if he could help me figure out what was wrong with her car.

I snuck out one evening while she was studying, telling her I was meeting the guys, and met Ash at Melanie's duplex. He checked her vehicle out, letting me know it was the starter. I had it towed to Ash's buddy's shop and secretly had it fixed. I really hope Melanie isn't pissed when she finds out. I read his message, angling my phone so she can't see it.

Ash: Hey Coddy. Car is fixed. I can drive it out tonight. Few of the guys are going to hit the rooftop bar, and Jaxon will give me a lift back.

Brady: Thanks man. I appreciate it. See you soon.

. . .

"Everything okay?" Melanie asks when I tuck my phone away.

"Few of the guys are going to hit the rooftop bar for a fast drink tonight. Join us?"

"Hanging out at a place I work on my night off." She taps her chin and laughs. "As lovely as that sounds," she says, her voice dripping with sarcasm. "I really do want to study. Friday will be here before we know it."

I lean in and give her a kiss. "I get it."

"Wait, if you're hitting the bar, does that mean we're not doing the ghost tour later?"

"Rain check?"

She nudges me. "You're making other plans because you're a scaredy cat."

I laugh and tug on her hair. "I am not a scaredy cat."

"Yes, you are. When you heard a 'bang' at Brighton's place, you came with a poker in your hand."

"Well yeah, but the point is, I came. I didn't run the other way." I nuzzle her. "I'm so glad I didn't."

Her breath is warm and sweet on my face when she gives a breathy little laugh. "Me too." We both turn our attention to the announcer as he makes a joke, and I lift my face to the sun, letting it warm my flesh as I admire the attractions.

"Look, that's King's Chapel cemetery. The oldest in the city and is a site on the Freedom trail. We'll have to check that out one of these days."

I nod, even though I don't much like graveyards. Just the sight of this one takes me back to when we buried my father. A wave of grief hits me, and I draw in a deep breath. Grief is a funny thing. You just never know when it's coming for you. That graveyard also reminds me of my own accident at sixteen and how I can't afford to be reckless. What if something happened and I couldn't be there to take care of my family back home?

What if they all got jobs and took care of themselves, dude?

After a while, we find ourselves in Beacon Hill, and Melanie nudges me. "Isn't it charming?"

"Wow, it really is." I take in the cobblestone streets, and the gaslit streetlamps and ornate ironwork doors.

"That's Acorn Street. One of the most photographed streets of Boston," she tells me as she pulls out her phone and takes a picture. "Takes you right back to Colonial Boston. It has everything one could want. Shopping, restaurants, and historic sites...some of the oldest cemeteries, although you might not like that," she teases as we drive by Louisburg square.

Is she pushing for me to get a place here? Maybe it wouldn't be so bad. The trolley turns and we find ourselves in a residential area. I know the area, as a few of my buddies live here, but it's not something I want. I don't think.

"Boston's oldest neighborhood," she says, giving me her own commentary as I consider the real-estate market. If I got a place here, Melanie wouldn't have to take the sublet and move into that pill box apartment that's going to squeeze her pocketbook. Is that why she's pushing? Is she thinking she might want something more permanent with me? The truth is, I can afford a place, I just never wanted the commitment or responsibility of owning my own house—for numerous reasons.

Why then, am I warming to the idea?

At that thought my heart thumps against my chest and Melanie's gaze moves over my face, her eyes narrowing in on me, like she can see more than I want. "I was only joking about you being a scaredy cat."

"I know," I say, even though I think she could be right. I'm in my twenties, and haven't been living because I'm too afraid of dying and letting down those I love. As I mull that over, I can't help but think how fucked up that is.

"This is fun, Lanie," I say and lean in and give her a kiss. She chuckles, and snuggles against me. We continue the tour and since we've been at this for hours, and it's time to head back home, we stay seated as the bus stops numerous times for pick up and drop offs.

It's nearing dinner time when we finally get off at the location where we were first picked up and I take Melanie's hand in mine as we walk back to our car. Clouds move in overhead and she glances at the sky.

I click the fob and my doors unlock as we approach the car. "I hope the rain holds off if the guys are coming over tonight," she says before she slides in.

I give her a wink. "Yeah, but if it rains, the night will be cut short and I can help you study, and maybe even put that rain check to use."

"You are a pretty good study partner and I've been wondering when we were going to use that rain check." She exhales, her smile fading. "I'll just be glad when this exam is over."

"You're going to do great." I bend and kiss her before shutting her door and circling the vehicle. Her eyes are on me as I walk, and I kind of like being the center of her attention. I climb in and as we head back to the resort, unease hits my stomach. Is she going to be pissed that I had her car fixed? Probably. But I guess I'll have to find a way to put a smile back on her face, and I'm pretty sure I know how.

"Why are you grinning?" she asks, breaking the quiet around us, and that's when it hits me. We can sit quietly together, zero conversation, yet we're completely comfortable. Normally when it's too quiet, I'll do or say something ridiculous to break it, uncomfortable with my own thoughts most of the time, but with her it's different.

I'm different.

"Thinking about chapter four," I tell her and she laughs.

"You young boys. That's all you ever have on your mind."

I wag a finger. "Hockey, don't forget hockey, and hey, I'm not that young."

"Younger than me."

"Does that bother you?" I ask, seriously.

"Last week in the coffee shop, that elderly lady you signed an autograph for asked me if I was your older sister."

"What, no way? You didn't tell me that."

"That's because it was embarrassing."

"I wouldn't have signed an autograph had I known she embarrassed you."

She shrugs. "She didn't mean it. She just saw you with those fourteen-year-old girls, and well, I'm no fourteen-year-old."

"First, let me say you're a gorgeous *woman*, and second, the fact that you have your life together and go after what you want, is pretty damn attractive."

There's genuine curiosity in her eyes when she asks, "That's why you like me?"

"I like you for many reasons. Not just because you're my... cougar," I tease.

She whacks me. "Ass, and really, Brady, when it comes right down to it, I don't have my life together. Not yet anyway."

"Not yet? You have a place to live lined up, you're getting the education you want. You have a job, and are making great tips to help with tuition, and...wait, what else do you want, Lanie?"

Her phone pings and she reaches for it, leaving my question hanging in the air. I grip the steering wheel tighter and curse at the emotions squeezing my throat—because yeah, maybe I wanted to hear that it was *me* she wanted.

She sends a message off and puts her phone down. "All good?" I ask.

"Yeah, just a classmate, asking about our exam."

I wait for a second, to see if she's going to answer my question, but the moment has passed. "Do you want to grab some take-out?"

"No, I think I'll cook, if that's okay with you." She's been doing a lot of cooking for me, cleaning too, and she's not my maid, but she does seem pretty insistent on it. "Healthier," she adds, as if to convince me.

"You don't have to cook for me."

"It's my way of thanking you."

"But you don't have to thank me. It's not tit for tat, Lanie."

"Fine, I don't want you to feel responsible for me."

What her eyes are saying is that she knows I'm responsible for everyone, and carry the weight of my family and my team on my shoulders, and she doesn't want to add to it.

Yeah, okay, I get it. We both have issues. What a fucking pair we make.

"Okay," I finally agree, because she's right. I'm in training and homemade is much healthier.

She hums to the radio as I drive, and about half an hour later, I pull up in beside Noah's vehicle. "I'm glad you had fun today, Brady."

"Thanks for dragging me."

She laughs and gets out of the car, and her jaw drops when Ash pulls up behind us in her car.

"What the..." She turns to me, eyes wide. "What did you do?"

I hold my hands up, palms out. "Don't be mad."

She glares at me. "You...you fixed it?"

I give an easy shrug. "Ash knew what the problem was and took it to his buddy to get it fixed."

"I...what did it cost?" Her brow furrows a worried expression moving into her eyes. "I'll pay you back."

"Okay," I say quickly. Not that I ever plan on taking the money.

"My car..." she frowns and glances down. "It's not your responsibility."

"Hey," I say and pull her to me, lifting her face to mine. "It's okay. You can pay me back. Any way you want," I joke.

Her frown deepens as she glances back down, and I dip my head to see her face. "Car's fixed," Ash says as he steps up to us and holds out the keys.

Melanie's gaze cuts to his. "Thank you. That was very kind of you. You didn't have to go to the trouble."

"No trouble at all and hey, any friend of Brady's is a friend of mine." Ash runs his fingers through his mess of hair and glances around. "The guys aren't here yet. We're supposed to meet for dinner."

Melanie grips the keys tight. "You're welcome to have dinner with us. It's the least I can do after fixing my car."

Just then Jaxon pulls in and parks behind Noah's vehicle. He hops from the car. "Hey guys. Where's Tuck?"

"Not here yet," Ash explains. "You still able to give me a lift back tonight?"

Jaxon grins. "Depends."

I laugh, because I know it depends on if he meets a hottie at the rooftop bar or not.

"Asshole," Ash says.

"I can give you a lift," I tell him.

Ash turns to Melanie. "Thanks for the invite. I'd love to take you up on it another night, but you don't want these assholes in your space. Let's go grab a beer, and I'm starved."

"I'll go start on dinner. You can join the guys if you want. I can reheat yours later."

"No, I'm coming." I brush my knuckles up against hers. "I'll meet up with them later."

She nods toward the door. "I'll head in then."

She walks away and Ash nudges me. "So, you and Melanie. What the fuck is going on there?"

I glance over my shoulder to make sure she's not within ear shot. "I'm helping her out."

"Yeah, with your dick. You two are obviously fucking."

"She needed a place to stay and who I'm fucking is not your business."

He looks at the house and then back at me. "Yeah, well, careful with that one."

"What's that supposed to mean?"

"Dude, you're in the prime of your life having a great fucking time with the bunnies. Women like Melanie aren't looking for a good time. They're looking for marriage, a house and kids. Ask Korbin. He got himself an older lady and now he's saddled with a handful of kids."

As far as I know, Korbin is in love and happy, but that has nothing to do with my relationship with Melanie. Besides she's not much older than me, for fuck's sake, and her biological clock isn't about to stop ticking... I don't think. "You have no idea what you're talking about."

"Yeah, well, when she convinces you to put a ring on it, starts pointing out houses she likes, and sells you on having kids, don't tell me I didn't warn you."

While I was warming to the idea of a house, the thoughts of a baby scare the shit out of me. The responsibility of a child is just too much. Not that I have to worry about that. Melanie doesn't want kids. She told me straight up, but I saw the look of longing on her face, which once again niggles at something in my brain. I might not be the psychologist here, but I don't have to be to know something is off.

16

MELANIE

I can't help but think it's been one heck of a crazy week with work, studying, and sharing a place with Brady, as I glance out the patio door to watch tourists soaking up the last of the summer sun with their families. Soon enough, they'll all head back home and the vibe will change. Busses will arrive with the retired crowd, and believe it or not, sometimes they can be rowdier than the spring breakers. I'm not complaining. The work and tips are going to go a long way toward tuition, and I've just about made enough to cover next term.

Thanks to Brady—and I do plan on paying him back—my car is fixed, and, also thanks to him, I don't have to make the commute back and forth to my place and waste a lot of time when that time could be put to better use, like sleeping in late with a hot hockey player.

But I was up early this morning, and sick to my stomach—not to mention a headache—worrying about my final exam which, according to the time on my phone, is less than two hours out. As I stand in Brady's kitchen, I take a breath and shake out my hands, working to expel the anxiety rushing through me.

"Hey, you got this," Brady says, coming into the kitchen. My heart leaps at the sight of him. Earlier, I enjoyed the sight of him too as he ran on the beach. Now he smells fresh and clean after his shower. He pulls me to him and plants a kiss on my mouth, and I've really grown accustomed to living with him—fast. I didn't really see him much this week, with me working and studying and him practicing. But it's Friday night, and he's insisting we celebrate after my exam.

"What if I don't got this?" How embarrassing would it be to go out for a celebration if I fail the damn exam.

"I've been testing you, and you're ready." He cocks his head. "Would I lie to you?"

"I'd hope not." He knows how I feel about liars and when it comes to trust, I don't take people at their word. I can't believe anything coming out of their mouths. I know better than that. Or at least, I used to. Until this guy named Brady Fisher—Coddy—nearly accosted me with a poker. He's a man who seems to keep his word, a man who gives without asking in return. Just look at what he does for his family— and I do hate how they all take advantage of him and how he thinks he's responsible for them when he's not—to the point he's almost terrified of really living because it could result in not being there for them. Wow, just wow. He's probably going to keep his word and do some big celebration, too, because he wants to do something nice for me—with nothing in return.

He laughs and whacks my ass as I go for another cup of coffee. He puts his hand over mine, uncertainty in his eyes. "Uh, maybe that's not a great idea. You're kind of jittery."

"You're right." I grab a glass of water instead, needing some-thing to wash down the bile punching into my throat. If I didn't have an exam today that was making me nervous, I'd think I was coming down with a virus. My stomach is achy and I'm kind of sweaty.

"Did you eat?"

"I had toast for lunch. I don't have much of an appetite. I'm sure I'll feel better once the exam is done. I get like this because I don't test well."

"What time do you want to leave?" Brady grabs a package of lunch meats from the fridge and opens it. The smell makes me a bit queasy, so I take a seat at the table and sip my water.

"I told you. You don't have to take me."

He shrugs, squirts some mustard on the bread and slaps down the meat. "I'm going into the city anyway. I have some things to do."

I eye him as he takes a big bite. "I don't want a big party or any kind of party for that matter, Brady." I warn and glare at him as I cross my arms. His face is full of innocence as he puts a hand on his chest and blinks at me.

"Really, Lanie." He scoffs and there's playfulness about him when he rolls his eyes at me. "You're such a narcissist, thinking everything in this world revolves around you."

"Fine, what things do you have to do?"

He walks up to me, and taps my nose. "Not everything is your business, either."

"You're infuriating."

He goes back to eating his sandwich, unfazed. "That's one of the nicer things people have called me."

Now it's my turn to roll my eyes. "Fine, if you insist on driving, let's head in after you eat. I wouldn't mind hitting up the campus community room and doing a few stretches and breathing exercises."

He gobbles up his sandwich, and nods. "Great idea." He pours a glass of water to wash down his sandwich. "Are you going in your pajamas or are you going to get dressed?"

"Right." I hurry to my room, pull on my most comfortable yoga pants and a T-shirt and shove a sweater into my book-bag. The air conditioning on campus is on full blast, and the rooms are freezing. Once I'm ready, I find Brady opening the door to greet Brighton and Camryn.

"What are you two doing here?" I ask. "I thought you'd be on your way to your summer home by now." They usually like to leave before lunch to beat the traffic.

Brighton rubs her protruding belly. "We weren't going to leave without wishing you good luck."

"Good luck, Ms. Melanie," Camryn says and wraps her arms around my waist.

"Thank you, Jellybean. Are you guys heading out now?" I ask Brighton, and her gaze cuts to Brady and they exchange a look I don't understand.

"Brady," I warn. "What is going on?"

"Nothing." He holds his hands up innocently.

"I have some errands to run," Brighton explains, and because she's not a very good liar, a good quality in my books, I know whatever it is Brady is up to, she's in on it. While I might be pretending to be mad about it all—I'm certainly not used to people doing things for me—it is rather sweet. Warmth spreads through my chest and it's kind of crazy because it weirdly feels like we're all just a big happy family.

Although that will end when my apartment becomes available. But I can't think about that right now, I have an exam to focus on.

"We're going to see Grandma and Grandpa," Camryn tells me.

"Oh, how lovely. Give them a big hug for me."

I cast Brighton a fast glance, and lower my voice when I ask, "Is everything okay?" Her mother-in-law has dementia and they have been trying to spend a lot of time with her.

"Camryn has some new artwork in her backpack and wants to share it."

Camryn holds her bag up. "Look, I have a backpack just like you, Ms. Melanie."

I tap her nose. "Yes, you do."

"Okay, go break a leg, Mel," Brighton says and leans in and gives me a hug. "Text me when you're done to let me know how it went."

"Will do."

They head down the stairs and Brady runs back to the kitchen to grab his thermos of coffee. A few minutes later I'm sitting beside him in his vehicle staring at the gorgeous ocean as he drives me into the city.

"I can see why you like living at the resort," I say with a sigh. "That view never grows old." He goes quiet, almost pensive, and I cock my head. "What, are you telling me you are growing tired of it?" He scrubs his chin and makes a snorting sound and my chest tightens. Okay, maybe it's not the view he's tired of and maybe he did lie to me a while ago when he said I wouldn't be a bother. Is he tired of having me around?

We've been having fun, haven't we? Sure, I've seen another side of him, a kind, compassionate caring side that he hides from the world, and I like that side. But maybe the loud obnoxious guy is who he really is and something about me stifles that. No, that can't be right. After learning about his past and his demons, I'm pretty sure I know who the real Brady Fisher is. God, I think I might have been confused for a moment there because I've been studying too long and now I'm projecting. And, of course, I can't forget that I still have a few of my own demons haunting me.

But if he is tired of me, I can't think about that right now. Again, all my focus needs to be on my exam and I'm going to clear my head and not delve into any kind of conversation that will set my brain off in a direction I can't have it going.

I go quiet and focus on my breathing as we drive and Brady falls quiet too, distracted by his own thoughts. Soon enough, he pulls up in front of my campus and I reach for my door. He touches my arm and leans in to give me a kiss.

"You got this."

"Thanks for the vote of confidence." He opens his mouth like he's going to say more, when someone calls my name and I look out the window to see Tania, a girl from my small study group, waving at me.

"Friend?" he asks, and I suspect that's not what he had on his mind.

"Tania is part of my study group."

"I didn't realize you had a study group, or friends on campus. You never mentioned them."

"I wouldn't exactly say she's my friend. We just all get something out of the study group. We all have different strengths when it comes to the material."

"Right, tit for tat," he says, scrubbing his chin, and it gives me pause. Brady swears life isn't about tit for tat, and not only does he tell me that, he's also constantly trying to prove it. I mean, how does it help him when he quizzes me? We might have played a sexy little game with it in the beginning, but I can tell he's very serious about my studies, and I love how he supports me. He's always insisting I don't have to cook or clean to stay at his place.

His family from Paradise, Newfoundland take horrible advantage of this good man, and his generosity, and I refuse to do that. I refuse to be duped by anyone ever again, which makes me keep everything I have close, and while we've both been taken advantage of, we now have very different outlooks on life.

The guy who borrowed the twenty dollars didn't dupe him.

"I better get going." He nods like he has a lot on his mind, and I open the door. "I'll see you in a few hours."

I hurry over to Tania, who is watching Brady drive away. "Ah, was that Brady Fisher?" she asks, sounding breathless.

"Yes, why?" I try to play it casual, but it's hard to do when her jaw is sitting on the ground.

"Are you freaking kidding me?" Her eyes are big and wide as

she watches his car disappear around the corner. "Brady Fisher, as in the goalie from the Bucks?"

"The one and only," I tell her and hike my backpack up higher. Trevor, another guy from our small study group, joins us on the path.

"What's that about Brady Fisher?" he asks and glances around. "Was he here?"

"Are you tapping that?" Tania asks and I shake my head and laugh.

"Tapping that?"

She playfully wags her eyebrows. "Okay, answering a question with a question now, are we?"

"Which means she's definitely tapping that," Trevor pipes in.

I start walking toward the building and the two fall in line with me. Trevor nudges me with his hip. "Just tell me you're using protection. That man has a reputation a mile long."

"That's not the only thing he has that's long," Tania says and my gaze flies to hers. She grins and puts her hand on my shoulder. "Or so I heard." She chuckles. "Might that be something you'd want to confirm."

"The only thing I want to confirm is we're all ready for this exam today."

Tania and Trevor exchange grins. "Confirmed," they both say in unison.

"Ohmigod are we fourteen?" I ask, exasperated.

"No but some of us are closer to it than others," Tania jokes, and while she's just kidding with me, it does remind me that I am older than Brady and that maybe he should be dating girls his own age. Why again is he with me when he could have any vivacious bunny he wants?

Trevor throws his arm around me. "Ignore her. She's jealous of your maturity and years of experience."

"Was that meant to be a compliment?" We reach the doors and Trevor opens them for us.

"Of course." He waves his hand for me to enter and I walk into the building. Students mill about as they get ready for their finals, and I excuse myself and head to the community room, where I do some yoga and center myself for the exam.

Ten minutes before it starts, I make my way to the classroom, and grab my usual seat. I'm pretty Zen by the time our professor enters, and when he gives us the go, we all boot up our laptops to take the online exam. Head down for the next couple of hours, I focus and begin to fly through the questions. When I come across a few essay questions from none other than chapter four, Brady's favorite chapter, I can't help but chuckle. A few heads turn my way and I refocus.

By the time the bell rings, I've answered all the questions and double checked most of them. I blow my hair from my face as I hit enter, and lift my tired eyes to find everyone else finishing up and powering down.

I catch Tania's eyes and she gives me a smile, then we both turn to Trevor, who is still running his fingers through his hair. I do the same when I'm stressed. "Trev, you good."

"Yeah, what are you guys up to now?" he asks.

Tania stretches her arms out. "I have a date with my bed. I plan to sleep for a whole week."

I groan with envy. "That sounds absolutely divine," I tell her, even though that's not in my near future.

Trevor hikes up his backpack. "You guys want to grab a beer first? Chill out for a bit?"

I hate to blow them off. I've barely seen them the last two weeks, but the thoughts of alone time with Brady is just what the doctor ordered to soothe my stomach and headache—well if I went to a doctor—which I didn't. "Can't. I have plans."

I stand and pack up my laptop. "Oh, do those plans involve Coddy?" Tania teases.

I lift my chin an inch and grin at her. "As a matter of fact, they do."

The three of us walk out of the classroom. "And might those plans involve a week in bed...but no sleeping?" she teases.

While that too sounds divine, I shake my head. "No, and I'm not sure what the plans are." I wince against the late afternoon sun as we exit the building, and my heart misses a beat when I find Brady leaning against his car waiting for me. I take a moment to admire the long length of him, the way his T-shirt stretches across tight chest muscles and how his shorts showcase strong legs and a trim waist. I wave and he pulls himself up to his full height and as he starts my way I run my palms over my mess of hair. "He's been helping me study all week, and wants to do something to celebrate, I just don't know what."

"Oh, wow, it's serious then?" Trev asks.

I give a fast shake of my head. "No, not at all."

They both look at me like they might know something I don't. "He helped you study all week..." Tania begins.

"...And now he's planning a surprise to celebrate," Trev finishes.

I give a curt nod, understanding how that could look to them. "Right."

Tania nudges me as Brady approaches, a big smile on his face and a fine shiver goes through me the way it always does when I'm the sole focus of his attention.

Trev leans in and whispers, "If that's not serious, then I don't know what is."

"How was it?" I ask, and lean in to kiss Melanie on her pale cheek, desperately needing the connection. Christ, what is wrong with me? I've only been away from her for a few hours. What the hell is going to happen when I'm on the road?

When our time together is over?

She stiffens a bit, a little uneasy chuckle catching in her throat. Is she embarrassed at the public display of affection? Does she not want people to know she's been sleeping with Coddy, the asshole with the reputation? I inch back, working to ignore the tightness in my chest as I take her backpack and shoulder it. Once again, embarrassment floods her face. Yeah, I get it, she's a girl who does everything on her own—a girl who is afraid to let anyone too close because it might end in hurt and betrayal—but she doesn't have to be tough around me. I want to help her and don't expect gratitude or anything in return, other than her happiness.

When you help your family, dude, you don't even get happiness from them. All you get is them wanting more and more and the only time they worry about you or your career is when it might affect their needs.

She folds her hands like she's not sure what to do with them and answers. "Not too bad. There were only a couple of questions I had trouble with, but I think I did good." Her eyes brighten, but beneath the shine, it's easy to see that she's worn out. She exhales and lifts her face to the sun, a hint of relief on her face. She's been working hard, and I want her to have some much-needed downtime before her next semester starts.

Her gaze flies back to mine and she shakes her head. "Where are my manners? I must be more worn out than I realize. Brady, this is Tania and Trevor. My small study group." Her brows scrunch together. "Although we haven't done much of it lately with me living in Sparrow Springs."

Students file out of the campus building and many slow to gawk at me as they pass, no doubt wondering if I really am Brady Fisher. I pull my hat down lower, not wanting to ignore them, but I'm interested in meeting Melanie's friends—or rather, not friends.

"We didn't know you moved," Tania says, not taking her eyes off me.

"Oh, just temporary. I have a place lined up for November."

She does, and the thoughts of her not staying with me leaves a hollow feeling in my gut.

I extend my arm to Tania and she greedily accepts my hand, shaking it enthusiastically as she steps closer. "Would it be weird if I asked for your autograph? I'm a big fan," she says.

"Not weird at all."

As she digs into her backpack for a pen and paper, I turn to Trevor and shake his hand. He sort of looks starstruck too. "Next game, why don't you guys sit in the box with Melanie?" Melanie's eyes go wide, because this is the first time she's hearing of the box—the first time I've invited her to a game. She'd gone a few times with Brighton in the past, but this time...maybe she's shocked because I asked.

"Are you kidding me? That would be phenomenal," Trev says, and slaps me on the back. "Is that okay with you, Mel?"

"Yeah, sure." She blinks rapidly, like she's trying to wrap her brain around this sudden turn of events. "Of course. I'll check the schedule against our next semester's courses and see what works."

"Hey, listen," Trev shades his eyes and looks down the sidewalk. "Mel said you guys might have plans later, but we were just headed out for a much-needed end of semester drink. Any chance you have time to grab one with us?"

"That sounds like a good plan. What do you say? Want to join them?" I ask Melanie as I wipe my brow with the back of my hand as the late afternoon sun beats down on us. "I could use a cold one and hey we need to celebrate."

She frowns. "Oh, I thought...um, yeah, that actually sounds like a great idea."

"I know a place around the corner," Trevor says and jerks his thumb out. "It's a Scottish pub called Kilting Around." He wags his brow playfully at Melanie, as if to entice her. "The guys don't wear hockey jerseys, but they do wear kilts. We could grab a cold pint there."

Tania loops her arm through Trevor's. "Hot guys in kilts and cold beer. I'm in."

They start down the sidewalk, and a warmth weaves its way through my blood as I take Melanie's hand in mine and she glances down as my palm swallows hers whole. "I'm so glad your exam went well. I know how stressed you've been. You put a lot of pressure on yourself."

She chuckles. "You're one to talk." She's right, I do put a lot of pressure on myself. I'm just better at hiding it than she is, and honestly, I don't want her to hide it from me. "Now to wait for the results." She winces like that might scare her, before she adds, "Did you get all your errands done?"

"All done," I say as we follow her friends who keep glancing back at me, like I might be a figment of their imaginations. They're friends—not friends—of Melanie's, so by proxy, they're friends of mine and I want them to see me as a regular guy, not an NHL player who's always loud and obnoxious.

Wait, did I just say I wanted them to see me for who I was?

I slow my steps to keep pace with Melanie's stride as she glances at me, her nose crinkled up in a cute way that makes me want to forget drinks and take her home, to bed. "You really want me to come to a game and sit in the box?"

"Sure, why not?"

"Because that's where the WAGs sit, and I'm not a wife or a girlfriend."

I look straight ahead, my brain racing. "No, you aren't, are you?" I say under my breath, thinking about how I can change that. I just don't want to scare her off if it's not something she wants. I know how hard she finds it to get close, and this arrangement came with a deadline that has been extended until she moves out in November. I spent the day moving pieces on the chess board, strategizing on how to extend it past that.

Christ, I have no idea what is going on with me. I have so many people counting on me back home, I never thought I could take on one more person, but it's different with her. Everything is easy with Lanie, which is probably why I continually drop my defenses when we're together. She doesn't make me feel like I *need* to be there for her—in fact, it's Lanie who wants to do things for me—and while it's always tit for tat with her, it does make me want to be there all the more, without wanting anything in return.

What is even happening in my life?

We reach Kilting Around and Trevor opens the door for us. I glance at the big sign over the door. How did they ever come up with the name? "I heard about this place. Just never been." I follow in behind Melanie and find a bunch of big Scottish men, full of tattoos, in kilts bustling about.

"I think I found my new favorite pub and study place," Melanie teases, and I playfully pinch her side.

"Hey," I tease, even though jealousy is zinging through my veins. We find a booth and slide in, and a server comes and brings us menus.

"Nachos for the table?" I ask.

Trevor and Tania nod, but Melanie puts her hand over her stomach. "I'm good. All the stress has gotten to me."

I put my hand on her knee under the table and give it a tender squeeze. "Still not feeling good?"

"It's anxiety. I get like this. I'm sure it will pass."

She really does put a lot of pressure on herself, and doesn't want to rely on anyone for fear of disappointment. "Okay." I shift closer, and offer my comfort and when I do I notice the longing in Tania's eyes as she watches us.

"I get like that too, Melanie," she says and wiggles in her seat. "The sight of our server looking hot in that kilt is helping ease my anxiety, though."

Trevor playfully hits her with his shoulder. "I saw him first."

"I think I might just get a soda," Mel says, as our server approaches us. I nod, and order nachos, a pitcher for the table and a soda for Melanie. Fuck, I hope she's not coming down with something. But if she is, tonight's plans will have to be put on hold.

I move my hand from her knee to her shoulders and pull her against me, kissing the side of her head. "Do you need anything? I can run to the drugstore."

"Thanks, but...oh wait." She plops her purse onto the table.

Tania makes a little *aww* sound as she watches me keep a comforting hand on Melanie. Melanie pulls some antacids from her purse and pops one in her mouth. "This should help."

The server comes back with our drinks and assures us our food will be out shortly. Trevor pours three glasses of beer and we all clink glasses to another semester done. I take only a tiny sip as I'm driving, but Melanie takes a long drink of her soda and moans in delight.

"Maybe I was just dehydrated. I'm already starting to feel better."

"So, why do they call you Coddy?" Tania asks.

With my arm still around Melanie's shoulder, I lightly play with her hair, and she groans and covers her face with her hands. "Oh God, don't ask."

"Oh, come on," I scoff playfully. "It's not so bad."

"Oh, this sounds juicy." Tania leans in, her eyes big and curious. "Now I really need to hear the details."

"Not juicy. More like slimy," Melanie says as she drops her hand, and I notice color returning to her cheeks.

My head rears back as I pretend to be offended. "I told you, they're not slimy, they're dry."

"Uh, what are we talking about?" Trevor asks, his stupefied gaze going back and forth between the two of us.

"Before he begins..." Melanie grins at me, and everything in her smile fucks me over in the best possible way. "Newfoundlanders are—"

"The friendliest people on the face of the earth." I nudge her. "Is that what you were going to say?"

She laughs. "Right, something along those lines." She holds one finger out. "Friendly." A second finger joins the first. "Eccentric."

"Eccentric?" I burst out. "How can you say that?"

"You have mummers, Coddy," she shoots back and turns her attention to her friends—not friends. "At Christmas time, they dress up and go house to house and sing and dance. The host has to guess their identity before offering food and drink."

"That sounds like fun." Tania flattens her hands on the table, excitement in her eyes. "I want to do that."

"I kind of do too," Melanie says, chuckling.

"How did you know about mummering?" I ask.

"I looked it up."

"Ah, doing a little research on me, were you, ducky?" I actually kind of like that she's interested in my heritage and culture.

"Just curious, *ducky*."

"Ducky is used for girls," I explain. "A boy is b'y."

Her shoulders relax. "Like I said, eccentric." I laugh as she grows animated, clearly having fun now as the stress of the day leaves her body. She holds out a third finger. "They call their kettle a slut."

"What?" Tania bursts out laughing. "That's it, from now on my kettle is a slut," she announces.

Melanie grins at me. "Go on, tell them how you got your nickname, Coddy."

The nachos come and I proceed to tell them about getting screeched in and kissing a cod, and Tania seems as disgusted by the whole tradition as Melanie. Trevor, however, thinks it's hilarious. We eat and chat and Melanie even has a few nachos. She eventually excuses herself from the table, and once she's out of earshot, I lean in and chat quietly with her friends, hoping to have a moment alone with them.

When Melanie comes back, she has a distrustful look on her face. "What's going on?"

"Nothing," I say quickly and sit back in my seat. She eyes me before turning her attention to her friends. "What's going on?"

They both shake their heads, and Tania checks her phone. "I have to get going. I...uh...have plans tonight."

"I thought you said you were going home to sleep for a week."

"Right." She shoves Trevor to get out. "That's my plan. Move it."

"Yeah, I have plans too. Gotta go."

Melanie shakes her head as I slide from the booth. "Jeez was it something I said?"

"We should get back," I say to her. "You're looking a bit pale again."

"Really." She puts her hand on her stomach. "I actually feel better after eating, and I didn't think I looked pale when I checked myself in the bathroom mirror."

"No," I say and glance over her face as I pull my wallet from my pocket, letting her friends know this was on me. I lean in and whisper. "You actually look a bit feverish. I think I might need to get you home to bed."

A quiver goes through her as she puts the back of her hand against her forehead. "You're right. I think I might be a bit feverish."

I turn back to drop the bills onto the table, and that's when I overhear Tania whisper, "Girl, he is so into you."

I chuckle, because yeah, it's pretty damn obvious. Hurrying my steps, I catch up with them and follow them outside. The sun is lower on the horizon, but we still have time for me to take her home and help her forget all about her day before I take her out for her end of the semester celebration. Something tells me she thinks drinks with her friends was her reward after all the studying and hard work, but no, she deserves more.

We head back to my car, and she smiles happily as we drive back. It's nice to see color on her face again. We talk quietly about my upcoming away games, and the house is quiet when we reach it.

I hurry from the car, cross the front and capture her hand when she walks up to me. Her smile is soft, and my heart jumps, wanting my mouth on her body, my cock inside her. Jesus, I've got it bad.

We head inside and straight to my suite. I shut and lock the door behind me, and silence hovers as I guide her to my bedroom. Once inside, I say, "I heard what Tania said to you when we were leaving the pub."

"What..." She swallows.

"About me being into you," I explain.

She gives a nervous laugh, like she's not sure what I think of that. But Christ, she must fucking know by now how much I truly am into her. Dammit, I'm not hiding the fact that I want to touch her all the goddamn time.

I angle my head and let it slowly move over her body. "She was right."

Desire floods her eyes. "Oh." She nibbles her bottom lip. "You're into me."

"Well, at least I'm going to be."

Desire morphs into confusion. "What?"

"Why don't you get on that bed, open your legs for me, so I can get 'into' you."

MELANIE

A bevy of emotions grip my throat as he looks at me with a dark intensity that warns he wants nothing more than to lose himself in me for the rest of the night. My heart misses a beat, because yeah, I can get behind that, or underneath that, or even on top of that.

Yeah, definitely on top of that.

I take a couple of fast breaths, my body aching, and wanting just that as I back up until my legs hit the bed. My chest rises and falls rapidly as sexual energy arcs between us. My God, the man is simply breathtaking, but it's not just the sex or his body that draws me to him, it's so much more, and well... that's a thought for another day, when I'm not the sole focus of his attention.

Desire flashes through me as he tugs his T-shirt off. My gaze drops to take in his abs as he pops the button on his pants and kicks them off. A moan catches in my throat as I admire his perfect naked body.

"Your turn," he growls.

I slide my finger into the band of my yoga pants and I wiggle, tugging them down just enough to tease him. He arches a brow, and I blink innocently. "Oh, you want them all the way off?"

"Off," he orders in a commanding voice that sends shivers skittering through me. "How else am I going to get *into* you."

Into me, right.

I swallow against a suddenly dry throat as I slide my pants lower. My stomach tightens, like it'd just taken an unexpected blow. *And why is that, Melanie?* Oh, I don't know, but maybe it's because when he said he was 'into' me, I thought he meant he was into me, like he wanted me for more than just sex. But as I look at him now, the need swirling in his eyes, it makes me question what's real and what isn't.

God girl, what a mess you're making of your life.

I wasn't supposed to open myself up to anyone or anything. Opening up only leads to getting hurt and I know that firsthand. My insides tighten as past memories come back to haunt me. Maybe it will be a good thing when his NHL season begins and I move out, because I don't know how much longer I can be around this man.

"Something on your mind, Lanie?"

My gaze jerks to his at the hint of seriousness in his voice and the words—*I'm falling for you*—dance on my tongue. *Girl, don't do it*. Do not tell Brady that you love him when he's only *into* you.

Wait, what did I just say?

Oh, just that you were in love with Brady Fisher.

Ohmigod, I'm in love with Brady Fisher!

Dammit, when did that happen and why didn't I better guard my heart? A sound catches in my throat, a half moan, half groan and I get it. There was no way to guard my heart against a guy like Brady. Dammit, I blame him for all this. He's the one who's constantly there for me, helping even when I don't ask for it, proving he wants nothing in return, and then he brings me into this house and shows me what a real family could look like.

"Lanie?" he asks again, a new kind of tenderness in his voice that simply draws me in deeper.

Feeling a little shaky, a little unstable, I swallow against the lump climbing into my throat, and try for playful. "Just thinking about how good your cock is going to feel inside me." I remove my yoga pants and underwear and his growl of appreciation rockets through me as I reach for the hem of my T-shirt.

He steps up to me, puts his hands over mine, and my mind shuts down. "Let's not keep you waiting." With a quick tug upward, he removes my shirt, and with one deft flick of his fingers, my bra slides from my shoulders. The man is talented, that's for sure. I lift my chin, meet his gaze, and the mixture of warmth and hunger I see there wraps around my fragile heart and squeezes tight.

His fingers curl in my hair, and his breath grows shallow as he takes my mouth with his. Heaven. That's what kissing him feels like. He slides his tongue in, and moans as his eyes roll back like it's the first time he's ever tasted me and I'm the best thing he's ever savored on the tip of his tongue. I kiss him, holding nothing back and that's when it occurs to me, the intimacy in what we're doing feels different, like this is the beginning of something special...something profound.

Like we're moving past sex and fantasies, into something far more important.

Honestly, I should be afraid, but as he touches me with tender concern, I'm not sure I can muster up my flight instincts. Actually, I kind of want to fight...for what's happening here.

Blistering heat explodes inside me as he slides a hand between our bodies and lightly strokes me. My body ripples and I rock into him, wanting more...everything.

A thick finger slides into my slickness, and my muscles clench around it. He moans against my mouth, and there's a great deal of tenderness in his eyes when he breaks the kiss, his gaze searching my face. "I love how you're always so ready for me."

Ready for him.

Oh, God, he's so wrong. I was never ready for a man like Brady.

He swirls his finger in my core, pressing deep into my body, leaving me aching and wanting, and searching for his cock. I take his thickness into my palm and rub from base to tip, and use the pre-cum spilling from his slit as lubricant.

I run my hand up and down, my mouth watering for a taste as I clench around his finger. As much as I don't want him to stop what he's doing, I need this man in my mouth. I'm almost desperate for it.

I inch back and confusion moves over his face, but it quickly morphs to pleasure as I sink to my knees and open my mouth for him. His moan fills the quiet of the room as he grips his dick and lightly settles it on the hollow of my upper lip.

I put my hands on his thighs and palm his hard muscles. "Are you into it?" I tease blinking up at him.

The need in his eyes hits me like a high voltage jolt, and my breasts grow heavy, aching for his mouth. "I'm into it, Lanie."

Is he talking about sex, or something else?

"Not yet you're not." I lean forward and take him to the back of my throat, reacquainting his cock and my mouth as he grips my hair, his body thrumming with need. His pleasure resonates through me and honestly, it's insane how close I feel to him in this moment.

I take him impossibly deeper and his fingers crush my hair, like he's doing all he can not to erupt in my mouth. While I'd like that, I desperately need his cock inside me. As if reading my thoughts, he inches back and leaves my mouth empty. I glance up at him, mouth still open, and he wobbles on his feet.

"Jesus, Lanie. How did I ever get so fucking lucky?"

My heart jumps, pounds against my chest as his words nearly knock the wind out of me. The last time a man made me feel this cherished this important was...well, the last time Brady touched me. A thrill heats my blood as I take him back into my mouth, and his legs wobble as I suck, his control nearly obliterated.

"Fuck," he curses, and takes my arm to pull me to my feet, only to give me a little push between my breasts. I fall onto the bed, my hair flaring around me, and he simply stands there, hovering, his eyes brimming with lust as he looks his fill.

I'm about to move, center myself in the middle of the bed, when he sinks to his knees before me and wets his lips. "All day," he begins, his breath warming my aching core. "All day, all I could think about was burying my mouth between your legs, and tasting you on my tongue when you come for me."

I wiggle and pitch my hips forward. "Let's not keep you waiting."

A chuckle rumbles in his throat as he grips my thighs, his fingers biting into my flesh as he widens my legs. He runs his nose along my inner thighs, breathing me in before he buries himself between my legs, my body trembling as his hot tongue laps at me.

I run my fingers through his hair and shamelessly move against his face as he eats at me. He growls and my blood ignites to a near boil when he puts a finger back inside me. I cup my breasts, toy with my nipples and fire licks over my body.

With his finger buried inside me, his mouth claiming my clit, the world closes in around me and I tumble into a powerful orgasm that wracks my body. He mumbles something from between my legs, and while I don't know what he said, from the deep growl in his throat, I'm sure it was something about loving the taste of me.

I grip the back of his head, fusing his mouth to my trembling sex as spasms of pleasure overtake me. He stays between my legs as I clench around his finger, and when the quakes stop, he inches back and our eyes meet. The second they do and I spot warm intimacy shining there, a new kind of warmth floods me.

I stand on wobbly feet, knowing exactly how and where I want this man next, and he nearly tumbles backward when our bodies collide. "Whoa," he mumbles, falling on his back-side and I chuckle and hold a hand out to him.

"Sorry."

His gaze moves up my body. "It's okay, the view is nice from down here."

"It's nice from up here too." He takes my hand and I'm about to help him up when he tugs me down on top of his body.

I moan and slip my legs around him. "Did you read my mind or something?"

"Nope, you're the head doctor, not me."

"Head doctor?" I laugh. "Is that what you think I am?"

"I think a lot of things, babe, and right now I'm thinking..." He pauses, puts his hands on my hips and easily lifts me. "... that you should fuck me."

I reach down, capture his stiff cock and hold it as he lowers me. "Oh God, Brady." I sink onto him, and he fills me, his crown hitting my cervix in a way that brings on a hard shudder. His hands move to my breasts, and he lifts himself up to take one nipple into his mouth.

"Mmm," he murmurs around my hard bud and sensations vibrate through me. His hands go to the back of my head as my nipple slips from his mouth and he brings my lips to his. There's something different in his kisses, his touch, the way his cock is filling me. It's intimate, tender, poignant. Then again, I just admitted to myself that I'm in love with him so it's possible I'm imagining it—wanting it—although I'm not entirely convinced this isn't real, or one-sided. Maybe that's why I'm offering myself to him openly, honestly.

I move my body, taking every inch of his hard cock, and press my hands to his chest, splaying them to touch as much of him as I can. We rock together, our eyes locked as we fly higher and higher. How the heck did I get here? I chuckle to myself as I sit on this beautiful man's cock—a man who could have anyone, but he's been pursuing me for a long time.

I close my eyes as heat floods my body and Brady groans as my orgasm approaches. He changes the pace, lifting me and pulling me down harder, faster until my muscles clench around his thick, pistoning cock.

"Brady," I cry out, giving myself over to this man in every way possible. The world closes in on me, and my head falls forward as lightheadedness overwhelms me.

"I've got you, babe."

His hands tighten on my hips and my heart thunders. He does 'got me'. In so many ways and for the first time in my life I feel so safe.

"Look at me."

I lift my head and meet intense eyes as he pulls me down, sealing us as one as he depletes himself in my body.

"Brady," I cry out again as his hot seed fills me and spreads heat, warmth and contentment through my body. I sit on top of him until he finishes spasming inside me, and when he stops, I fall forward and rest my face on his chest. His heartbeat is strong as it pounds against my chest, and there's just something so darn comforting in that.

We stay like that for a long time, until my legs begin to go numb. I roll off him and wince as his cock leaves my body. Suddenly chilled, I grab my discarded T-shirt and cover my upper body. He rolls, pulls me against him and warms me with his hot flesh. I'm not sure if I'm imagining this new closeness between us as we snuggle, but I really like it. I lift my head to see him. "That was a great way to end a long hard day."

"Speaking of long and hard," he teases, and feeling playful, I reach between our bodies.

"Nope, can't find anything long and hard here," I tease.

"Is that right?" He rolls on top of me, and gives me a kiss so soft and tender, I melt under him. "I'm hungry."

I cock my head. I was expecting a sexual comeback following the teasing. "I can make us something."

He pushes my damp hair from my forehead. "No, you had a long hard day."

"And a long hard evening," I add with a laugh.

He nods and glances at the window. "But it's still early. Let's go out and grab a bite to eat." As he eyes me, I wipe a sheen of moisture from my forehead. Am I feverish? "Are you okay?" His eyes narrow. "Headache back?"

"No, not at all." If the man wants to go out and eat, then I'm not going to let anything stand in the way. "I'm hungry too." At least, I think the gurgling in my stomach is from hunger. I didn't eat much at the pub.

"What do you feel like?" he climbs to his feet and holds a hand out to me. I take it and he pulls me up beside him.

"A shower."

He chuckles. "Good idea." Hand in hand, we walk to the bathroom, and we take a luxuriously hot shower together. Once we're done, we head back to the bedroom and I pull on a pair of clean yoga pants, a T-shirt and a loose-knit sweater. He dresses in jeans and a polo shirt.

Ten minutes later, I'm sitting beside him in his car, and he's driving back toward the city. I have no idea where he wants to eat, and I don't much care. I'm just happy we're together.

"Oh hey, when I was doing a little research on Newfoundland." He arches a brow. "I told you I was curious about your strange traditions." I grin and add, "Anyway, I read that the government is going to be expanding and upgrading the fishing plant. Lots of new employment opportunities will be available."

His head rears back, confusion on his face, and something tells me no one in his family mentioned that to him. "Really?"

"Yeah, and isn't that fantastic? That will bring a lot to the communities." He nods and goes quiet, and I change the subject. "Thanks for keeping my end of the semester celebration low key," I tell him as he drives. "It's what I wanted." Honestly, I'm surprised my pants aren't on fire. Jeez, I really have no right to feel sorry for myself, especially after that amazing, intimate sex.

It's true, I told Brady I didn't want anything big, or anything at all. Yet, deep inside me, I kind of hoped he'd do something special. God, haven't past lessons taught me not to set myself up for disappointment? But that's exactly what I did and I have no one to blame but myself for the way I'm currently feeling. A groan catches in my throat and I quickly disguise it with a cough.

"Dry throat," I explain.

"I can stop and get you something to drink."

"No, I can wait."

See, right there. His thoughtfulness. How could I not fall for a man like Brady? Yeah, this is definitely all his fault.

He takes my hand and squeezes it and I lay my head back and let my lids drift shut as he drives. A short while later, he pulls into a parking spot in the downtown core and I sit up and glance around.

"Where are we?"

"You'll see."

He jumps from the car, circles it and opens my door. I take his hand and join him on the sidewalk, glancing up and down the block in search of restaurants. We walk down the sidewalk and he stops outside what looks like a small house, but the bottom level is a business. I glance up and read the sign. *The Nook.*

"The Nook." I'm pleasantly surprised as I question him. "This is the café that Gina owns? The woman we met on the beach, and I made a virgin daiquiri for her daughter?" He nods and I ask. "This is where you want to eat?"

"Yes, but it's also where I wanted to have your celebration."

He pulls open the door and tears fill my eyes when I see Brighton, Noah, Tania, Trevor and a bunch of the guys on his team, along with their wives and girlfriends.

"Don't be mad," he says quickly.

Mad, how could I be mad? This once again proves he's a man who keeps his word and I can't believe he went through all this trouble. Why would he do that?

Why am I even asking myself that? This is Coddy, and he doesn't ask for things in return. "I'm not mad, but... Brady, I...I..." I shut my mouth. I don't want to lie to him and tell him I didn't want this. It seems like he can see right through me anyway. My gaze goes to Gina as she comes towards me, a huge smile on her face and a beautiful cake in her hands.

Brady leans in and whispers. "She jumped at the chance and went out of her way to help me organize all of this. No catch, Lanie. I think you two are going to be great friends."

Friends...

I warm to that idea as Gina shows me the cake. God, I don't know what is wrong with me. I'm not usually this emotional. But today has just been...so amazing.

"It's beautiful, thank you."

Gina's smile widens. "I'm so happy you like it."

I turn and cup Brady's face. "Thank you."

His grin is mischievous. "Don't thank me yet."

I frown and eye him as a bunch of his teammates cheer behind me. I turn in time to see Conner and Ash coming toward me with a great big... Is that a cod?

Brady wags his eyebrows. "Time to get screeched in, Lanie."

"No," she yells and stumbles backward, landing right into Brighton, who laughs as she catches her. Melanie turns and gives her friend a hug, and Conner stalks toward her, taunting her with the big fish.

"Conner, get away from me," she yells, and whacks at the fish, although it doesn't appear she has any intentions of touching it. "That thing is disgusting and is only going near my lips if it's deep fried and served with a side of fries." She glares at me, and while she's feigning outrage, there's warmth, playfulness and genuine happiness dancing in her eyes. "This..." she huffs out, and steals another fast glance at the fish. "This is my celebration? This is what you had planned?"

"You said you weren't mad."

"This is crazy." Her words are saying one thing, but that smile on her face tells me a whole other story. She loves this and maybe the fact that I'm asking her to be an honorary Newfoundlander holds a lot more meaning than I'm letting on.

I angle my head. "You're not going to do it? Not ready to be a Newfie?"

She arches one brow and folds her arms across her chest. "Wait, didn't we agree that I already kissed the cod?"

Whistles and back slapping erupt around us as the guys jostle one another, totally getting the gist of it. I shrug. "I once tried to give you an out, but nope, you said that was cheating and lying, so the only way you can become an honorary Newfoundlander is to actually do it. This is kind of on you, Lanie."

She laughs and shakes her head at me, but seeing her this happy totally fucks me over.

"Do it, Melanie," Gunter yells.

She points to him and laughs. "You do it."

Big-ass cod still in hand, Conner turns his attention to Brighton. "How about you, Brighton?"

She backs up into Noah's arms. "Come near me with that thing and I'll be making deep fried fish and chips with your..." She glances down. "Well, you know."

"All right, give them a break." I wink at Melanie again. "For now."

Melanie shakes her head. "I need a drink."

Gina sets the cake down. "Right this way." Gina threads her arm through Melanie's and Melanie grabs Brighton.

"Screech is over here." I say as Ash hands me the bottle.

Everyone laughs as I crack open the cap. Melanie glances at me over her shoulder and smiles. I smile back, and can't deny that there's something very different about her tonight. Hell, there's something very different about me, too. Up until Melanie, I tried never to let myself feel and when I did, I hid those emotions behind a veil of sarcasm and humor but feelings aren't so scary when I'm with her.

Conner backs up, turns the fish toward himself, puckers up and gives it a big sloppy kiss.

"Ohmigod, Conner, you're disgusting," his sister-in-law Dani says and cringes. He jokingly grabs her, and tries to put his fish lips on her cheek, but she whacks him and runs to Melanie as Gina pours them all a glass of wine. Man, I can't believe I pulled this off without Melanie finding out. I had everyone in on it, and thought the perfect place to celebrate was at Gina's new café, so Gina could meet new people, and Melanie could see just how many friends she really has, how many people really care about her.

Tania and Trevor walk over to me, and they both look so starstruck with so many players from the team here. Trevor slaps my back. "Thanks for the invite. I don't think I've ever seen Melanie surprised before."

"I think I'm going to pay for this later."

Tania laughs. "If you're lucky." I laugh with her and she scans the room. "I think I've died and gone to heaven." Her mouth drops. "Is that..." Her words fall off as her brain stalls.

"Elias, yeah. Nice guy. Why don't you go say hello?"

Taking deep breaths, she grabs Trevor's arm. "You come with me in case I stumble over my words."

"Like I'm not going to stumble over mine. Jesus, that man is hot."

I turn as a few more guys arrive, most of them alone, but a few of them with dates. I smile. It's kind of nice to have this get together before we hit the ice hard for the season. I search out Melanie again, and while I'm excited about our upcoming conditioning camp scrimmage, I'm going to miss her like mad. She's laughing with her friends and they all keep glancing at me. I'm not sure what they're saying, but she does have a mischievous gleam in her eyes.

"So, what now?" Conner sets the fish onto the big tray, and wipes his mouth with the back of his hand. "Aren't I supposed to drink something?"

"Actually," Melanie says coming toward us with her glass of wine. She shoves it against Conner's chest and he takes it. "You did it wrong. You drink and then you kiss the cod. So, you're not an honorary Newfoundlander, Conner, and if anyone here is going to be an honorary Newfoundlander, it's going to be me."

My jaw nearly drops to the floor. What the hell had come over her in the last five minutes? I'm not sure but I like it. I like her. "No way."

Her chin lifts an inch and bobs it. "You don't think I'll do it?"

I love the challenging way she's bobbing her head, and looking at me like she wants me to dare her, which reminds me of our game of truth or dare. I still owe her a truth. Should I tell her the truth of how I'm feeling? Is that something she might ask me?

"No, I'm pretty sure you'll do it."

The guys start chanting, "Do it. Do it!" and I pour her a shot glass of screech. She takes it from me and lifts her arm, raising her glass.

"Is ye an honorary Newfoundlander?" I ask and when she eyes me, I lean in and whisper, "This is where you say, "Deed I is me ol' cock, and long may your big jib draw!" She laughs, and recites the words. I nod toward her glass. "Now shoot it back."

She shoots it back and winces like she's drinking paint thinner and when she pounds the empty glass on the table and smiles at me, pride fills my soul. I crook my finger, and Conner picks up the cod and holds it out.

"Now ye kiss the cod."

She briefly closes her eyes, takes a deep breath, and gives the big ugly cod a kiss on the mouth. Cheers erupt and she throws her arms around me, pressing her fish lips to mine, but I don't give a fuck.

I inch back and she asks, "What exactly was it that I said?"

I put my mouth close to her ear my words for her alone. "Just that every wish I make is yours to command. Apparently, you are now my sex nymph, Lanie."

She whacks my chest even though her cheeks just turned a pretty shade of pink. "Stop it."

Chuckling, I tell her the truth. "It means, yes I am, my old friend, and may your sails always catch wind."

She looks around. "Aren't I supposed to get a certificate or something?"

Gina holds a piece of paper in the air and the crowd parts for her. "Right here."

Melanie laughs and throws her head back. "You really thought of everything, didn't you?"

"I'm a guy who follows through, Lanie."

Gina hands me the paper and a pen, and I fill in Melanie's name. "Where on earth did you ever get that cod?"

"It wasn't easy." I hand her the paper and hold a hand out to shake hers. After the shake, I lean in and kiss her and a few people tell us to go get a room and I'm pretty sure that's not a bad idea. She puts both arms around me and presses her lips to mine.

When she breaks the kiss, she inches back. "Brady, I lo—" her words die abruptly as she glances around, like she'd forgotten we were in a crowd of people. "I love that you did this."

Was she going to say she loved me? Jesus Christ. Does sweet Lanie Clark love me? Is that what I want. I have so many people relying on me, but dammit, I want this. Deciding to play it cool, I pull her against me.

"Glad you love it."

"If I didn't like you before, I sure would now."

It's crazy to think I asked her out many times and she said no. It took my friends going away and me thinking she was a burglar to bring us together. Did Noah and Brighton set that up? I'm not sure, but if they did, I'll have to thank them. "I like you too, Lanie." She smiles at me and something inside me gives. Fuck it. I cup her face, my heart pounding in my chest because dammit, I'm going for it. "That's a lie," I tell her.

She blinks rapidly. "It's a lie?"

"No, it's not a lie. I do like you...but..." I take a deep breath as emotions flood my body and this time, I don't suppress them. "I love you, Lanie."

She gasps, and tears pool in her eyes. "I...I love you too, Brady. I wanted to say it. I almost did, but I didn't know."

"You love me?" I ask like a fool as an exuberant childlike laugh—a sound I'm sure I've never made before—bubbles up in my throat.

"Yeah, I do, and when we get home later, I'm going to show you how much, just like you showed me how much you loved me earlier."

I capture her lips with mine, and kiss her with all the love exploding inside me. Nothing in my life has ever felt so good or so right. I've been so afraid for so long that I haven't even been living. I've been hiding.

Music begins playing and she wraps her arms around me and we hold each other like our lives depend on it as we sway to it. We dance for a while, and when Gina starts bringing out hor d'oeuvres, Melanie breaks away.

"I should go help."

"It's your party." I take her shoulders and guide her to a table. "Gina, you've done enough, too. Have a seat. The guys and I will get the food and drinks."

She looks perplexed. "Are you sure?"

"Sit," I demand in a playful voice. She nods and drops down next to Melanie. Brighton and a few of the other women join them. Tania and Trevor are too busy chatting it up with Elias to even notice anyone else is in the room.

"Conner, Gunther!" I yell. "Come help me in the back."

I turn to spot Conner off to one side, no longer joking and happy. His head is dipped and he's in deep conversation with Dani, and for a second, my muscles tighten. I can't hear what they're saying, but from the looks of it, it seems pretty intense. What the hell? I know they have history and hang out a lot, but Conner is big into the bunnies. Wait, I haven't seen him with too many bunnies lately. Is there something going on between him and his sister-in-law?

"What's going on there?" I ask Gunther as he walks over to me.

He turns to see what I'm looking at. "No clue, man."

"Ash, give us a hand," I say when he starts walking by.

We all head to the back of the small café and step into the tiny kitchen. I pull open the fridge and find trays of food.

"Who's this Gina chick, anyway?" Ash asks.

"Melanie and I met her one day on the beach. She inherited this place and is pretty new to Boston."

"She's kind of hot," Ash says and jokingly sticks a toothpick into one of the meatballs and holds it up to examine it. "And I do love a woman who knows how to handle balls." He tosses the meatball into his mouth and moans in appreciation.

"She's a mom," I quickly inform him.

"Oh," he blurts out, stepping back like I was about to light him on fire. He holds his hands up, palms out. "Kids change everything."

"Yeah, they kind of do," I agree. That thought suddenly sours my stomach. I know in my heart that deep inside Melanie, she wants kids of her own. Fuck, there's no way in the world I'd want a kid ever counting on me to be a parent.

Gunther takes one of the trays from me, a grin on his face. "So, you and Melanie, huh? You're pretty into her, aren't you?"

"I like her." I'm not about to tell him that we're in love. It's new and exciting, and I want to keep that inside me for a little while longer.

"But the real question is, do I owe you another?"

"What are you talking about?"

"Double or nothing remember?"

"What?" I take another tray of food and hand it to Ash.

"You got her into your bed, so I owe you a beer," he explains. "Now do you owe me a beer because she didn't fall for you, or do I owe you two?" He angles his head. "I actually think she did fall for you, and I owe you two."

Knowing he's joking and ignoring that, I zero in on 'fall for you' comment. "You think she's fallen for me, huh?" I ask, keeping the private words we spoke private.

"Oh, yeah, big time, dude."

"You looking for me?"

I turn at the sound of Conner's voice and when I find him standing there with Dani, who has a worried look on her face, my stomach tightens. Did she overhear Gunther, and if she did, does she think he was serious?

MELANIE

It's been one glorious month since Brady told me he loved me, and I revealed the same to him. Honestly, things have been going well with us. We haven't talked much about my living arrangements, probably because he's been so busy with hockey, and I've been trying to work and go to classes. But I still have my sublet for November and it's probably best I keep it.

Right now, the thoughts of packing and moving sounds exhausting with this relentless headache. I haven't been feeling all that well these last couple of weeks, and have missed far too many shifts at the bar, which isn't going to bode well when tuition is due next month. I don't know what is wrong with my stomach or my head. I was sick last month at the end of exams, and can only blame this new virus on the stress of a new semester and a busy fall season at the resort. Not to mention our living arrangements and our future together.

Here it is, late Friday morning, and for the first time in a while, my stomach feels a bit better, but my head, not so much. Unfortunately, I don't have a shift at the bar tonight—the one night where I'm sure I could make it—and while making money would be nice, I'm also happy to go out to dinner with Brighton this evening. It's been a while since we've had a girls night out. I'm just not sure I should eat or drink much. I don't want to set my stomach off again.

As I glance out the patio window, I note the dark clouds overhead. It doesn't matter. The view of the water and beach never gets old, even when it's raining. I'll have quite a different view when I move to the city, and that's okay. I really enjoy being in the city and close to all the amenities. I'll be farther away from Brady, for sure, but we can make it work. With love, anything can work, right?

I do wonder how long Brady will live here, though. At some point, won't he want his own house? I think deep down he's afraid to spend money, with the way his family takes advantage of him, but it's not my place to say anything more. We're only dating. It's not like we're married and I have any kind of say. I'm also not his therapist.

I check the time on my phone and throw my laptop into my backpack. I have a class after lunch, and need to get moving, although I don't have to take the bus or train and that's a blessing. I still can't believe Brady went to the trouble of getting my car fixed. I haven't paid him back yet, and he doesn't want that, but I feel like I need to. It's still so hard for me to let go of past trauma and realize the man wants to do nice things for me—without anything in return. How did I ever get so lucky?

I rush to the bathroom to comb my hair and groan at the dark circles under my eyes. I've been sleeping, a lot actually, but I can't seem to get caught up. If I didn't know better, I'd think I was pregnant, but I'm not. I had a period a couple weeks ago. I shudder at the thoughts of pregnancy, despite the small part of me that totally adores Camryn and Gina's daughter Zoe.

Gina and I have gotten to know each other over the past few weeks and she's become a good friend. The trouble she went through to host a party for me touches my soul and warms my darkest corners. It's crazy to think how far I've come in the last few months since meeting Brady. Other than Brighton, I really had no friends.

I pull on a nice pair of jeans, and a blouse, since I'm going out to dinner right after class and want to look nice. Once I'm satisfied with the look, I pick up my backpack and walk to the door. Just as I'm about to open it, my phone pings and my heart jumps when I see it's a video call from Brady. I quickly pinch my cheeks to add color. He knows I haven't been feeling all that great lately, and that I've been missing shifts and I don't want him worrying about me any more than he already does. Like I've said, he has enough responsibility with his family as it is.

"Hey Coddy," I tease playfully when I see that he's in his hotel room. "Alone?"

"Yeah, Nicklas just left. Are you headed out?"

He sounds so tired. I hope I didn't give him whatever virus I'm fighting. "On my way to class."

"Sorry I would have called earlier, but I didn't have any privacy."

"Were you hoping to catch me in bed?" I tease.

His grin is wicked and playful. "Would you hold it against me if I said yes?"

"Are you talking about my body?" He laughs and runs his hands through his hair, and I can tell he's getting into goalie mode, trying to focus his thoughts for his game today. "How do you feel? Are you ready to kick some New York butt? I really wish I could watch you. I've never been to New York."

"We'll come on vacation one of these days," he assures me.

A little thrill goes through me. "I like the idea of that."

"Maybe an after graduation celebration."

I laugh at that, but the idea that he's planning long term makes me happier than I can put into words. "You're too much, Brady."

His eyes narrow and I almost pull the phone away. "How are you feeling? Still tired?"

"Jeez, thanks," I shoot back, playing it off. "Tell me I look awful without telling me I look awful."

"I'm sorry, babe." He frowns and blinks, looking completely sincere and apologetic for hurting my feelings.

"I'm kidding," I hurry out, appeasing him. "I'm okay. I was just up late studying." Not a lie. I wasn't well enough to work last night, so I opened the books and fell asleep on them.

He eyes me like he's not sure he believes me, then he lifts his head and glances at something in his room. He seems distracted. "I better get going."

"Have a great game." I blow him a kiss. "Sending all the positive vibes."

"Love you, babe."

"Love you too."

He frowns for a second and I don't know why but a burst of unease moves through my veins. He looks like he wants to tell me something, but isn't sure how. "Brady?"

He blinks, and focuses back in on me. "Have a great day, and see you tonight."

"Okay. Talk soon."

I end the call and step into the hall. I hear little Camryn laughing from her wing of the house and a small pang of envy tightens in my stomach. My God, what is going on with me? I swore a long time ago that I'd never bring kids into this world, but I never thought I'd be in such a loving relationship either—with a guy who is adamant he doesn't want kids either. Maybe I'm emotional because I'm missing him so much.

I push those thoughts to the back of my brain and hurry down the stairs. Outside I walk to my car as more dark clouds move in and I hold out my hand, catching a few light drops. Even though the air is colder, I enjoy the cool drops on my flushed face.

In the car, I turn the music on and enjoy the drive into the city. Once I reach my campus, I park and instead of going to the library to review my notes before class, I head to the financial payment office, to get my final payment invoice.

"Hey, Jenna," I say to the elderly lady behind the counter. I've gotten to know her over the years, as she's helped me with my payment plans. Her smile is bright and contagious as she pushes her glasses up and grins at me like she knows a secret I don't. "Do I have food on my face?" I swipe at my mouth and laugh. Maybe she's noticed the dark circles under my eyes, but surely to God that wouldn't make her smile.

"What are you doing here?" she asks, and picks up a pile of papers and shuffles them to straighten them into a nice, neat pile before she slips them into a manila folder.

"I wanted to get a printout of my last payment."

She angles her head. "You're all caught up, sweetie."

I stand there for a second and then glance over my shoulder. Is she talking to someone behind me? Since no one is standing there I turn back to her. "What are you talking about?"

"Your final tuition has been paid in full."

"That can't be right." I point to the big monitor in front of her. "You'll have to check again."

"Do you want to pay it again?" she asks, in a teasing singsong voice.

"No, but I mean, there has to be a mistake." God, it can't be paid. There's obviously a mistake and I need to get to the bottom of it. Can you imagine if I didn't pay because of a mistake and ended up not graduating?

"Honey," she begins and leans forward. "One very hot hockey player came in here the other day and paid off your balance. If I were you, I'd be hurrying home to thank that big hunk of hotness."

My blood drains to my toes and I grip the counter. I'm not sure if I'm lightheaded because I just found out Brady paid my tuition, or if it's because of this damn persistent headache.

Jenna's smile collapses. "Honey, are you okay?"

"Yeah, just fighting a flu." I push off the counter. "Thank you." My knees are wobbly as I walk down the hall and find the library. My brain is still racing as I drop down into a chair and pull my phone from my bag.

Brady paid my tuition? What the hell?

As I try to wrap my brain around that turn of events, I slide my finger across my phone, ready to call him and yell at him. Lord knows I don't want him to feel responsible for me, but I pause, because he's currently preparing for a game. Could this be what he was trying to tell me earlier? Maybe he knew how I'd react and didn't want to say anything before his game.

I set my phone down, deciding what I want to say in a conversation for when we're in person. I mean, I *am* touched by his generosity, but it also upsets me. I don't want him to feel like I'm his responsibility. I would have found a way to make the payments. I always do. It's just been a little harder with the missing shifts.

In the library, I try to study, but can't seem to focus, and when it's finally time for class, I pack up and walk down the hallway, meeting up with Tania and Trevor. They're still talking about my celebration party at the Nook. I try to stay engaged and not distracted as we talk, and soon enough, I take my seat in the class.

The professor, who I adore, seems to drone on a little bit longer today, and by the time he's finished my appetite is back, the muffin I'd eaten for breakfast doing little to sustain me through the day. I hurry from the lecture hall once he finishes and make my way to the bathroom to fix myself up before meeting Brighton. Since makeup is doing little to hide the dark circles, I head back to my car and drive to the Italian restaurant Brighton chose. Apparently, she's been craving pasta.

Rain is falling hard by the time I park, and since I didn't have the foresight to bring an umbrella, I'm pretty soaked by the time I make it to the restaurant. I glance around inside and I'm a bit surprised to see that Brighton has brought Dani along.

The hostess leads me to the table, and Brighton jumps up to hug me. But then she pulls back abruptly. "Are you okay?"

I use the rain as an excuse. "I know I'm a mess. I forgot my umbrella."

She smiles, and waves her hand toward Dani. "I hope you don't mind that Dani is joining us." Dani gives a feeble smile, like she's worried I could be upset that she's here.

"Of course not. I'm so glad you could join us, Dani."

"Thanks. With all the guys away, Brighton asked me to join you both."

I drop down next to Brighton at the table, and the server comes. Since Brighton is pregnant, she orders a soda, and since that sounds good to me, I order the same. Dani, who appears to be nervous about something, asks for wine. I think she could use a glass or two. I don't really know much about her, and I don't really understand her relationship with Conner, other than she was married to his late brother.

"Dani was just telling me about this hot book she's reading for book club."

"Oh yeah?" I take a sip of water. "I can't wait to read a book that doesn't involve psychology. Honestly, I'd love to lose myself in a novel."

We talk about books for a few more minutes. The server delivers bread, and butter and our drinks. The sudden smell of fresh bread, which I freaking love, turns my stomach and I lean back in my chair.

"Whoa, are you okay?" Brighton asks.

"I don't know. The smell of that suddenly made me queasy."

Brighton rubs her big belly, her voice joking when she teases, "Maybe you're pregnant."

A strange, garbled sound catches in Dani's throat and both Brighton and I turn to her. Heat flushes her face as she looks at everyone and anything but me. "Are you okay?" I ask. Maybe she's the one who's pregnant.

Dani reaches for her glass of wine and takes a gulp. "Yeah, bread. Just choked a bit. I'm okay now."

We stare at her for a second and when she doesn't say more, Brighton turns back to me. "Wait, you're not pregnant, are you?"

I laugh and shake my head, because that's seriously ludicrous. "I'm not pregnant," I assure her, and give her a dismissive wave of my hand.

She lets it go, and after the bout of nausea passes, we have a nice evening chatting. The rain has lightened by the time I leave, and I give my friends a hug before I head to my own car. I jump in and drive toward home. As I pass a drug store, Brighton's words jump into my brain and I slow the vehicle.

Should I get a pregnancy test?

My phone pings as we pull into the driveway, exhausted, sore and in a bad fucking mood after losing to New York. I pull my phone from my pocket as Noah kills the ignition and reaches for the handle, no doubt anxious to get inside and see his wife and child.

I glance up at the window and see the lights burning in my wing of the house. Melanie texted me a few times and I kept my answers short and sweet. She doesn't need to know how fucking shitty I feel for letting my team down. Christ, how that last winning goal got by me... I'm going to play that shit show over and over in my head all night and I don't want to subject her to my sour mood as I beat myself up.

Noah's about to get out of his car, but stops and turns to me as I stare at the message from my mother. "It was only an exhibition game. We'll kick their ass during the regular season."

Emotions are a weakness, Brady. You're the man of the house now, so grow a set.

As my mother's words suddenly come back to haunt me, I laugh—like I always do—and shrug. "Yeah, I know, man. It's all good." He eyes me. What the fuck? I've always been able to hide behind my humor and sarcasm. Being with Melanie is changing me, and I'm not sure if it's for better or worse, because dammit, I don't want my team to see me as weak. The truth is, I take this game very seriously, and tonight I let Coach and the guys down. Every time I do that, it cuts me to the core.

But are emotions really a weakness, Brady?

Maybe they're not. Maybe that's what Melanie has been trying to show me, but right now, I can't get out of my own head to even work through that.

"You coming?"

I shake my phone. "I have to send a message. I'll be up in a minute." He pauses for a second, and I toss him a grin. "Go see your wife and kid, dude."

He nods and exits the car and I let loose a long breath as I stare at Mom's text, asking for more money. My stomach clenches and a new kind of anger bursts through my blood. I'm about to text back, asking how much, when my phone rings. I guess I took too long to answer.

"Hey Mom."

"You're not answering your texts?"

"I just got home from an exhibition game. I was about to answer you." I pinch the bridge of my nose as one of the lights in my living room brightens. Melanie is up there waiting for me and I'm a real asshole to keep her waiting. "Did you catch the game?"

A pause and then, "No. I've been down and out, Brady. These pills I'm on are making me dizzy."

The pills she's been on for as long as I can remember...and the booze.

I glance out the window, stare at the trees blowing in the light breeze as my chest tightens. "Okay, no problem."

"Why haven't you sent the money for the new SUV?"

Jesus.

"I'm not a goddamn ATM," I blurt out without thinking.

Mom gasps. "What the hell, Brady? You might not be a goddamn ATM, but you'd be nothing without me. You owe me."

The thing is, I always felt like I owed her. But what about me, my life, my future? I haven't fucking been living.

I hear a rustling sound and Uncle Wayne's voice comes over the phone. "What the hell has gotten into you, son?"

The blood in my veins freezes. "I'm not your son."

"You ungrateful little bastard," he yells. "Who do you think you are?"

"I think I'm Brady Fisher."

"Brady Fisher, who's forgotten where he came from."

A disgruntled laugh bubbles from my throat as I say, "Oh, no. Trust me. I've not forgotten where I've come from. I know exactly where I've come from."

"What the hell you getting at, b'y? You some big shot now? Living in the big city, and think you're better than the rest of us."

Bile punches into my throat. "It's not that."

"Oh, probably got a new fancy house and car. Can't help family anymore."

"Wayne…what's wrong with the last vehicle I bought?" I ask. "It's only two years old."

"Why are you questioning me? You don't believe we need a new vehicle."

I open the passenger side door and step into the night, letting the cool air wash over me. "It's just a question."

"Since when did you start questioning things?"

"Since now."

"If you need to know, Carl needs a new vehicle. I'm going to give him that piece of shit you bought two years ago."

Piece of shit?

Gravel crunches beneath my feet as I walk aimlessly. "Maybe Carl should buy his own vehicle."

"What's he saying?" I hear my mother yell out, and then muffled sounds come through the phone.

"What's going on with you, Brady?" Mom shouts into the phone.

"I'm just wondering why Carl can't buy his own vehicle."

"You know…he's…he's out of work." Her words come out a bit slurred.

"They're upgrading the processing plant, new technology, new jobs. Maybe he can get work there. Maybe Uncle Wayne should check it out, too."

A gasp of outrage rings in my ear. "Are you saying you're not going to help?"

I've never said no before, never questioned anything. I just buried shit down and did what was expected of me, but I'm fucking tired of it. "I have some things on the go." I'm not going to abandon my mother, but I need her to understand where I'm coming from, and I hope like hell she supports me. "I'm trying to save."

"Oh, what? You got some bunny pregnant or something?"

Okay, I guess she doesn't understand or support. Nice. "No."

She gives an almost hysterical laugh. "Careful, b'y. One of those bunnies will latch on and take you for everything you got."

Is she talking from experience?

I pace back to the car, and lean on the passenger side door, which I'd left open. "I think Carl should apply for work at the plant, and take care of his own family," I state, hardening my voice to make my point perfectly clear. "I can't support them anymore."

She makes a tsking sound. "You're such a disappointment," she says quietly, clearly changing tactics with me. "Might as well have died when you got in that accident when you were a kid, for all the good you are to me now."

My heart hammers so loud, I can barely hear myself think. I pull the phone from my ear as she yells and I toss it onto the driver's seat and close the door, done listening. My legs are shaky as tears pound against the back of my eyes, and for the first time in my life, I'm not sure I can keep them contained.

Jesus Christ. I can't let anyone see me like this.

With no place to go, I start toward the water, but there are people out walking and I don't want anyone to recognize me. The last thing I want is a conversation. I walk by the stairs to the rooftop bar, and since it's closed, I figure maybe that's a good place to hang out and chill for a few minutes.

I take the steps two at a time and when I reach the top and find gate locked, I simply jump it. The lights are off on the pool and I walk around it. Maybe I should go for a swim. I circle it a few times and drop into one of the lounge chairs as tonight's loss and my conversation with my mother and uncle race around my brain like hamsters on a wheel going nowhere.

Fuck.

I look back toward the house, knowing Melanie is waiting. Jesus, she deserves better than a guy like me. This is how I get after every loss, and yes, I love the woman, but do I want to subject her to these kinds of moods. Maybe if I let myself experience more emotions, I'd get better at dealing with them.

I lay flat on my back as the quiet of the night surrounds me but does little to quiet my racing mind. Dark clouds part and make way for stars to shine bright, and that's when I realize the chair I'm on is soaked. I still don't move. I'm not sure I can.

As worry, responsibilities and failing to win tonight's game weigh me down, a creaking noise grabs my attention. In the dark of the night, I turn toward the gate as someone opens it and enters the pool area. What the fuck? The place is closed for the night. Is someone robbing the place? That thought takes me back to the night I nearly poked Melanie.

I lie perfectly still, wanting to fade into the black, to disappear into the night, as footsteps sound on the pool deck. Rustling sounds behind the bar followed by slight cursing sounds reach my ears, and I sit up a bit straighter. That's when my chair creaks and a small gasp, followed by stillness and silence curl around me. I hold my breath, not wanting to draw any attention to myself when Melanie's voice fills the quiet.

"Is someone there?" She asks, and as the moon shines down, I spot her inching toward the gate. Shit, I scared her.

"It's me."

She stops moving, speaking. Christ, is she even breathing?

"Brady?"

"Yeah."

In the darkness I see the silhouette of her moving toward me. "What's going on? What are you doing out here?"

"I guess I could ask the same question." *Way to deflect, dude.*

"I was looking for antacids. I knew we had some behind the bar."

Worry invades my gut, and I shift, throwing both legs over the side of the lounger. "Why do you need antacids? Are you okay?"

"I have indigestion." She closes the distance between us. "Are you okay?"

I open my mouth to tell her I'm fine, that the world is fine, that I'm living my best life, only to close it again. Who the fuck am I kidding? She can see right through me, but I don't want to bring her down.

"You should go."

"Brady." Her voice is thick, layered with concern as she drops to her knees in front of me. She cups my face, and when I try to pull away, she won't let me, and fuck, maybe I don't want her to let me. "Why are you out here hiding?"

Jesus, this woman is astute. I scan her face in the dark, and the concern there wraps around my heart and squeezes tight. "We lost."

"I know. I watched the game."

As soon as the words leave her mouth, I nearly fucking sob. I haven't known this woman intimately for all that long, yet, unlike my family, she watched my game. "I let the team down and I don't want them seeing me like this. I don't want them to think I'm weak."

"No, Brady, no. You are not weak, and you did not let your team down. Besides, being upset or showing emotions doesn't mean you're weak."

I shake my head, ignoring that last part as she holds me tight. "You said you watched the game. You saw the last goal I let in."

"Oh, Brady, babe. No. You are not responsible for your entire team. You're a team. You all win as a team and lose as a team, and it wasn't even really a loss. It was just an exhibition game. You can't beat yourself up over this."

I go quiet for a long time, and her hands leave my face and slide around my neck. She brings me to her, and I rest my face against her chest. Something about her strong heartbeat does something to me, has me opening up in new ways.

"My mother..." Her hand goes still on my back. I wait for her to speak and when she stays quiet, I continue. "She called me tonight. Wanted money for a car. It's a long story, but basically told me I might as well have died all those years ago because I'm no good to her."

Air leaves her lungs and washes over my neck as she inches back to face me. "I'm sorry, Brady. You don't deserve that."

I shrug, not sure if I do or not. "When I was growing up, after we lost Dad, she told me I had to toughen up because I was the man of the house."

"You were only eight, right?" I nod. "No eight-year-old is the man of the house Brady."

I shrug again. "She's pretty fucking mad at me." I search Lanie's face, and she stares back with a raw concern that means a whole fucking lot to me. My heart pounds and I take a minute to pull myself together before I speak again. "My uncle basically accused me of thinking I was better than them."

"I haven't wanted to say much, Brady. Lord knows we all have our demons, and I'm not saying anyone is better than anyone else. But let's face it. They do nothing when work is available, and they expect you to pay for everything. You train hard for your job, play even harder during games. You help everyone out at every opportunity, and yes, I know about my tuition and no, I'm not mad because I know you did it out of love, and you never want anything in return. Maybe that does make you a better person."

"I don't know." I force a smile, and lightly brush her hair from her face. "I'm glad you're not mad."

"You've come a long way, not because of your family, but maybe despite them," she whispers, her voice low, like she's trying to soften that harsh truth. I remember saying something very similar to her once. "Trust me, I know all about that."

This time I cup her face. "I know you do." I give a tortured laugh as my love for this woman pushes back the pain.

"They're grown-ass adults, Brady. You are not their meal ticket and they are not your responsibility. Just like winning and losing with the Bucks is not all on you. You have to let that belief go. I know it's ingrained, and I know it's going to take a lot of work to move past that, but I'm here to help you find a way forward and build a life for yourself if you let me."

She's saying everything I never knew I needed to hear. "Thank you."

"I had to walk away from my family and the situation I was in for my own mental health and growth. I'm not saying you need to do that, Brady. But you do need to set boundaries, and stick to them."

"You're right. I do." I take a deep breath. "I love you, Lanie."

"I love you too." She lightly presses her lips to mine before her lips quirk into a playful smile. "Parents... they can really fuck a kid up, huh?"

Again, I know she's talking from experience and she has come such a long way. How could I not love and admire a woman like her.

"Yeah," I snort out. "All the more reason I'm never going to be a father." She inches back, her movements stiff, like my words just pierced her heart.

Was it something I said?

22

MELANIE

I roll over in bed, and reach for Brady, only to find out he's not there. I sit up, a little panicked as my heart thumps. Last night, I'd never seen him so hurt, and it still breaks my heart to think his mother said such cruel words to him. He was only standing up for himself, and while it's great to help out family, there is a line in the sand, and they've crossed it too many times.

I listen for sounds, and when my ears are met with silence, I push the covers off and walk to the window, expecting him to be out for a morning jog and that's probably good for him. As I search the sand, and find no traces of him, my hand goes to my cramped stomach. Another wave of panic moves through me.

The other night when I was out with Brighton and Dani, I did stop at the drugstore and pick up a pregnancy test. I didn't take it, because I'm one hundred percent sure I'm not pregnant. Heck, I had my period not long ago. Okay, maybe I'm ninety-nine percent sure I'm not pregnant, and maybe I should take the test to confirm it.

Lord knows I don't want to be having a baby, especially after last night. I can't even imagine what Brady would do if I had his child growing inside of me. He certainly made it clear that he never wanted to be a father, and yes, I've told him there was no way I was bringing children into the world either.

I push that from my mind, and stand, going to the closet to grab my old but fluffy robe. I don't have a lot of clothes, and when I went back to the apartment to get my things—when I knew my roommate was gone—I only had a bedroom full of personal things to bring. I didn't have to haul a bed. Not because Brady had one, but because the place was furnished, just like my sublet is going to be furnished.

I walk to the kitchen and the delicious scent of hazelnut vanilla coffee reaches my nostrils. Brady must have already made a cup, but where the heck is he? I inhale as I put a pod into the machine. I spot movement on the patio and walk to the door. My insides soar when I spot Brady, leaning against the rail. God, I love that man so much it's insane.

I note that he's dressed in jeans and a T-shirt, ready for the day, as I slide the door open. He turns, and I'm surprised to see his phone pressed against his ear. Something moves into his eyes when he sees me—something that looks like annoyance, irritation even— and he gives me a curt nod. That's when it occurs to me, he doesn't want me in his space right now. He turns his back to me, speaking quietly into the phone, his words for the listeners ears only.

Is it his mother again? Anxiety grips my stomach, and I swear if she hurts Brady again, I'm going to have words with her. But right now, his words aren't for me, so I inch back to give him privacy.

The coffee machine finishes and I grab the milk out of the fridge. I pour it into my cup and don't know why I'm suddenly feeling rejected. That man is allowed to have private conversations that don't involve me. I take a much-needed sip of coffee and I'm about to take it back to the bedroom, to give him even more privacy, when he steps into the kitchen.

"Hey, sorry about that." He steps up to me, puts his arm around my waist and gives me a tender kiss that eases some of my worries.

"Everything okay?"

"Yeah, I ah. I just had some things to deal with." He must read the worry in my eyes, because he continues with, "No, it wasn't Mom. I don't think I'm ready to talk to her just yet."

I go up on my toes and kiss him again. "You know I'm here if you need to talk or work anything out."

"Thanks, babe." He checks his phone and frowns. "Listen, I have to go to town. I have some errands to run." I'm about to tell him I can shower fast and join him when he inches back and scrubs his face, glancing around like he's searching for something. "How's your day looking? Studying?"

Ignoring that pang of rejection again, I blurt out, "Oh yeah, always."

"Okay. I'll catch up with you later then?"

I nod, and he steps from the kitchen, leaving me there with my coffee, concern and confusion about what the heck is really going on. Where is he rushing off to in such a hurry, and who was on the phone?

Nope, don't go there, girl.

The man is allowed to have a life outside of me, plus I really should go over yesterday's notes and I do have to work tonight. Yes, Brady paid my tuition, which helps ease my financial worries, but I'm not going to slack off on work, and I'll pay him back one way or the other, because that is going above and beyond what a boyfriend does for his girl.

A little jolt of excitement wells inside me. I do like being called his girlfriend. I roll my eyes so hard, I nearly give myself a headache. *Get it together*. I'm a grown woman, not a love-struck teenager.

I leave the kitchen and walk into the living room, dropping down onto the sofa. I stare at my backpack, but I'm not really in the mood to pull out my laptop. Brady comes from the bedroom, sliding his wallet into his pocket and heads toward the door.

"I'll catch up with you later. Maybe we can go out to dinner?"

"I work tonight, remember? I'm not off until eleven."

He frowns and glances down. "Oh, right."

What is going on with him? Why does he seem so ruffled and out of sorts?

"I can make us dinner," I offer.

"I'm not sure what time I'll be back. I'll text you, okay? I can grab take-out for us. Maybe Thai?"

The thoughts of Thai food, which I usually love, suddenly turns my stomach. "Sounds good," I tell him, not wanting to worry him about my health when he clearly has something very important on his mind.

"See you later. Good luck with studying today." His phone pings, and he pulls it from his pocket to read the message.

"Oh, I might be grabbing a beer with Conner and Gunther later." Then just like that, he's out the door. I sit there for a moment, hear his car rev in the driveway and then stand to get my day going. I'm not one to mope around, and I'm sure if something horrible was going on in his life, he'd share it with me, right?

I finish my coffee and take a quick shower. Maybe I'll check in with Brighton after lunch. I could take Camryn to the park, to give her a break, and I still owe her for letting me crash at her place that weekend when she was away. That's when I remember it's Saturday and she's headed to their summer home.

Feeling an odd bout of loneliness, I dress in comfy yoga pants and a T-shirt and since I have no appetite, I go to the sofa and boot up my laptop. I study for a while and it's well after lunch when I lift my head, deciding I should put some food into my stomach. I head to the kitchen to eat. The second I crack an egg into the pan, nausea overtakes me, and I turn off the burner. What the heck is wrong with me?

Maybe you should take that test, Melanie.

Ugh. I push the pan to the back burner and walk into the bedroom. I tug open my nightstand drawer and dig out the test that I had buried under all my lotions, pens and notepads. I hold it for a second. This is stupid. I can't be pregnant. I open my phone and check the dates. I know I had a period like two weeks ago.

Just do it.

I walk to the bathroom, and even though I think I'm being ridiculous and over cautious, I decide to pee on the damn stick. Once done, I set my phone to chime in three minutes, and I pace up and down the hall. When I'm writing an exam, three minutes goes fast. When I'm waiting on a pregnancy result, it's the longest three minutes in the world.

My phone finally chimes and I hurry to the bathroom. I pick up the stick, expecting to see negative results when two of the biggest, pinkest lines I've ever seen kick me in the gut.

What the ever-loving hell?

I take two fast breaths, sure this is a mistake. I sink to the floor and grab the pamphlet, reading it for the second time. But there's no mistake about it. Two pink lines means I'm pregnant. But how, when? The room closes in on me and I pretty much catch my breath. Seconds turn into minutes, and I have no idea how long I've been sitting on the floor when I reach for my phone, although I don't even know who to call.

A car outside draws my attention, and I jump up and run to the window in time to see Noah pull out of the driveway, Camryn in the back seat. That must mean they haven't left for the cottage yet and Brighton could still be home. I hurry to my door, tug it open so hard it hits the wall, and bolt across the hall. I knock hard, and hear Brighton call out, telling me it's open.

I fling the door open and when I enter, she's nowhere to be found. "Brighton," I practically yell. "I'm pregnant."

She comes from the kitchen, a cup of coffee in her hand as her eyes go wide. "What did you say?"

I hold the stick out. "I'm...pregnant. Two pink lines. Ohmigod, how did this happen?" I begin to hyperventilate, and she comes hurrying over. She sets her coffee down, puts her arms around me and rubs my back as she leads me to the sofa.

"It's okay. We can figure this out."

"No, we can't," I shriek. "This is bad. Ohmigod it's so bad. Brady...oh, God, Brady. How can this be real?"

"Did you have a period?"

"Yes." I pause and think about it. "I mean I was spotting, and I figured that was my period. Sometimes when I'm stressed, my periods get messed up. I'm on the freaking pill, Brighton." I take it regularly." Wait, did I miss a day or two when studying? Oh God, what is happening in my life.

Brighton lifts her head, and looks toward the kitchen, her lips twisted in worry. I follow her gaze and that's when I spot Dani standing there. Oh, shit. I didn't know she had company and I certainly don't want anyone knowing my private business.

"I should go." I'm about to jump up when Brighton puts her hand on my leg to stop me. "No, you should stay. I think there's something you need to hear."

My gaze goes from Brighton to Dani back to Brighton. Brighton frowns and I'm guessing whatever it is she needs me to hear, I'm not going to like. "I'm having a hard time believing it," she begins quietly. "I mean, I know Brady quite well and this doesn't sound like him, but Dani overheard something that night at your party. It's been eating at her, and she came here today to talk to me, trying to figure out what to do."

By now my heart is in my throat and a new kind of panic overtakes me. "What's going on?" Dani drops down next to Brighton, her bottom lip red and raw from chewing on it. "Dani?"

"I didn't know whether to say anything or not, but now that you're pregnant, I think you need to know."

Heart beating so hard against my ribs, I lean forward and hug myself, but there was nothing I could do to brace myself, or prepare for what she said next.

"You were a bet, Melanie. I'm so sorry."

"A bet?" I grip the stick tighter, nearly snap it with my hands. "I don't understand."

Dani swallows and glances at Brighton, who gives her a nod. Brighton turns back to me and takes my hands in hers.

"I overheard Gunther and Brady talking about double or nothing." I lean toward Dani, her voice is so low I can hardly hear her. "Gunther said he owed Brady a beer because he got you into his bed. Then he said something about him owing Brady another beer for getting you to fall for him."

I sit there, blink once, twice, three times as her words bounce around inside of my brain, making no sense at all. What is she talking about? I was a bet…and the prize was a beer? No, she must have heard them wrong.

"Melanie, are you okay?" Brighton's voice cuts through the confusion in my head.

"Yeah. Sure. I think you must have heard them wrong, Dani."

Dani and Brighton exchange a glance and I push to my feet. "I need to go."

"Melanie, please. Don't go. We need to talk."

I have no idea how my wobbly legs carried me to the door, but the next thing I know I'm back in Brady's suite, staring up at the ceiling from his bed. Soft knocks sound on the door, but I ignore them, and when Brighton texts, I message back that I need some alone time.

Brady was meeting the guys for a beer...

I wrap my arms around myself. A bet would explain why he was with me when he could have his pick of women. I take deep gulping breaths, as my mind goes through everything, from the first time we met, to this morning, when he was completely distracted by something. As old insecurities creep back in, I can't seem to push them down. I lay still for a long time, my thoughts a chaotic mess, and when I hear the front door open and Brady call out to me, worry in his voice, I force myself to sit up.

Why is there worry in his voice? Does he know that I know?

He calls out to me again, and when I don't answer he eventually checks the bedroom. "Hey," he whispers, crossing the room to sit next to me, but I scoot to the other side of the bed, and force myself to my feet.

"What's going on?" He stands and walks to the end of the bed. "Brighton texted me, told me I needed to come home. Are you sick?" His gaze moves over my face. "You're pale again."

Unable to help myself, I blurt out, "I'm pregnant."

Blood drains from his face, leaving his skin a greyish white color. He falters backward, his eyes wide with shock, surprise...disbelief.

"You're...pregnant?" His gaze drops to my stomach. "Is this a joke?"

"No."

His gaze cuts back to mine, and there's a new kind of hardness there, and accusation in his glare raises the hairs on the back of my neck, "You said you were on the pill."

A crazy sound bubbles up in my throat. "I was...I am," I shoot back.

"Lanie, what the fuck is going on? How could you be pregnant if you were on the pill?" He goes quiet and scrubs his face, and I try to examine the barrage of emotions hitting him. Confusion. Disbelief. Anxiety. Fear.

Understanding.

His eyes lift, and there's a different kind of hardness there now, and that's when I realize his demons have come back to haunt him too.

"Holy fuck. You weren't on the pill. You did this on purpose. You wanted kids, didn't you?"

I briefly remember the way he reacted when I told him I was on the pill to regulate my periods. There was a moment of hesitation, like he wasn't sure if he believed me. "I didn't do this on purpose." I'm not sure he's even registering what I'm saying as he begins to pace. "Do you really think I'd lie about being on the pill?"

His voice lacks emotion when he retorts, "You've lied about things before."

"Are you kidding me." My heart jumps into my throat. I can't believe he's bringing up the money I hid from my parents. "You're bringing that up," I yell.

He shakes his head with disgust. The weight of his glare sits heavy on my shoulders. "Jesus. Fuck. I was warned about this."

My head rears back. "You were warned about this? You were warned that I'd get pregnant?"

"Yeah, the guys warned me you were probably looking for a baby, because you were older than me and were no doubt looking to settle down."

"The guys told you that?" I run a shaky hand through my hair. "And you believed them?"

"I saw the way you looked at Zoe on the beach, the way you are with Camryn." A derisive snort fills the air. "I used to wonder what was holding you back, what was missing from your life that was keeping you from having children, but I guess now I know."

I fold my arms as my body begins to shiver. "Do you now? Then why don't you enlighten me."

He snorts again, and backs away from me. "The only thing holding you back was a sperm donor. Fuck, you wanted something from me, just like everyone else in my life."

I fight back the tears. He doesn't deserve them. I work not to sound as shaky as I feel. "Wow, that's what you think of me?"

He turns toward the window and I take in his stiff shoulders as they curl up to his ears. "I can't have a baby, Lanie." Fear reverberates off every word and heightens the anxiety coursing through my veins. "I can't do it. I can't take on that responsibility. I told you that."

"Is that it, or was I just a bet to you?"

He turns fast, his jerky gaze back on my face as his body stiffens. "What?"

"I was a bet." I glance at his bed and call on calm, even though there's a storm going on inside me. "A beer to get me into your bed." His body is practically trembling when I turn my focus back to him. "A beer to get me to fall in love with you. Is that where you were today, out collecting your wins?" He opens his mouth and I hold my hand up to stop him. I'm not nearly done. "I get it, Brady. I told you a long time ago everything was tit for tat, and you just proved it to me once again." Despite my best efforts to stay calm, a hysterical little laugh bubbles out of me. "I live here, you get sex in return, and a nice cold beer to wash it all down. Fantastic. Well done." I clap my hands.

"Lanie, it's not like that."

I arch a brow. "Truth or dare."

"What?"

"Truth or dare," I snap again. He cocks his head and I explain, "You still owe me a truth from our previous game, and you should probably stick with that because I don't think you'll like the dare."

He exhales hard, and runs his hand through his hair. "Truth."

"Did you make a bet with the guys? Was there beer involved?"

"It was a joke."

I shake my head as my heart crumbles a little bit more. "Is everything a joke to you? I thought you were something different. I thought you were someone more. I thought we had a real connection. But maybe I should have stuck with my first impression of you. Maybe that's the real Brady, and this new, kind, tender, sweet version you presented to me, was just the Brady who was trying to get into my pants and my heart."

He starts to come my way but I back up and he stops. "Lanie..."

"Did you make the bet? Remember, you picked truth."

He looks down, shame reddening his face, telling me all I need to know. "Yes, I made the bet, sort of..."

I don't think sort of counts. "If you picked dare, I was going to tell you to leave, so I can pack my stuff in private. I think that still stands."

"Lanie, wait please. Don't do this."

I gulp as hurt rakes down my throat, making speech painful. "It's okay, Brady. I got your sperm, remember. So, I don't need you anymore now, and if you had to rush home before you got to have that beer with the guys, maybe now is a good time to rectify that."

He stares at me long and hard, until his expression shuts down. I finally find the strength to turn my back on him. A moment later, his footsteps sound on the floor and the front door opens and closes with a slam. My entire body shakes, tears flooding my face. I sob like a toddler and sink to the floor, my legs too weak to even hold me up. I cry for a long time, until a soft voice pulls my attention.

I glance up to see Brighton. "I heard Brady leave, and let myself in. Don't be mad." She sinks to the floor with me, taking my hands in hers. "Talk to me, Melanie."

Before I even realize what I'm doing, I'm talking non-stop, blurting out everything that happened since Brady first found me in her apartment and nearly poked me with the fireplace poker. I spill it all, leaving nothing out, and I cry the entire time.

Once I'm done, Brighton grabs a few tissues and wipes my face. "Do you know what I'm hearing?"

I sniff and take the tissue from her. "What?"

"That you two love each other very much."

"I was a bet to him, Brighton. He was using me, and trust me, I've been used enough to know it when I see it."

"Okay, I've given this some thought, and Noah and I have talked, so let me ask this: why would the man throw a wonderful party for you, get your car fixed, pay your tuition, and bring you into his home when you needed out of yours?"

I crush the tissue in my hand. "To make me fall in love with him. To win a bet."

"Deep in your heart, Melanie, do you really believe that?"

I sniff and bend my knees, bringing them to my chest. "Yes," I answer half-heartedly.

"I don't know a lot about your past, but I do know there was trauma. Do you think you're still clinging to that and expecting the worst from everyone, never taking anyone at their word?"

"I...I don't know."

"I've seen the way Brady was with you. I've seen the way he looked at you. He was tender, caring and loving. I don't think those things can be faked. You brought out another side of him. A good side. A great side. He's a wonderful man with a huge heart. Not many people get to see that side of him."

"He said...he said, I used him for his sperm."

"He was reacting. He might be a great man, but underneath it all, there's so much vulnerability. I know you see it too. He obviously has a lot of work to do on himself. I think you know that."

Her words ping around in my brain for a long time, and when I realize everything she's saying is right, I let loose a garbled laugh, the knot in my chest loosens. "Who's the psychologist here, anyway?"

She squeezes my hand, her expression pained. "Which brings me to my next point." I arch a brow and she continues, "If a client came to you and said everything you just said to me, what would you tell them?"

Fear erupts inside me as my brain races. "I would tell them to unpack the past, deal with it and then leave it there, otherwise they can't move on to a happy and healthy future. I'd tell them that things in the moment are often said out of fear and trauma." I take a couple of deep gulping breaths as my words sink into my own brain. I glance around the room and feel Brady's absence like a deep ache. "Oh, God, Brighton. I've made such a big mistake."

"Okay, so then maybe for the first time in your life, it's time to take your own advice."

23

BRADY

I've been driving around aimlessly for hours now, my thoughts a chaotic mess as my painful conversation with Melanie plays out on repeat in my mind, until I don't know what's up or down anymore.

Melanie is pregnant...

My God, I can't be a father. What the hell do I know about raising a baby, and don't I have enough responsibility as it is? What if I fuck the child up? Or worse. What if something happens to me and I can't be there for them?

I take deep gulping breaths, and when I nearly rear-end the guy in front of me, and car horns start honking at me, I pull over. That's when my phone rings, and I snatch it up to see that it's Noah. I stare at his number and debate on answering. I'm not much in the mood for conversation, and I'm sure he's fully aware of what's gone down by now, which means a lecture is incoming—and deserved. Fuck, I can only imagine that he's going to tear me a new one.

And why would he do that, Brady?

Oh, because of the way I reacted and handled the situation.

How did you handle it, dude?

Like a goddamn asshole.

I have no doubt he's going to yell at me for the things I said to Melanie, and for making a stupid bet in the first place. What was I thinking? I might have been joking with the guys, but Melanie was never a bet to me and I can't even imagine how much that would have hurt her. But fuck, she didn't believe me when I tried to tell her the truth, and after getting to know her, I can totally understand where all the distrust came from.

You didn't believe her either, dude.

Jesus, do I really think she's the type of girl to trick a guy? No, I fucking don't, and yeah, I lashed out, because I've spent a lifetime with others taking things from me, using me for what they want—I can see that so much more clearly now, thanks to Melanie—a woman I've really hurt. A tortured groan rumbles out of my throat. Deep in my heart, I know she's not a woman to take advantage of anyone. Which is why I want a future with her, and why I left the house early today. I didn't want to just tell her how much I loved her. I wanted to show her.

Yeah, you did a real good job of that, asshole.

Oh God, what the fuck have I done?

I start breathing so hard and fast, I begin to hyperventilate. Even if I went to her now, no way is she going to forgive me for the things I've said, and I'm not sure she'll ever believe she was so much more than a bet. Trust is hard for her, taking people at their word even harder, and I fucked all that up. I pound the steering wheel, my chest rising and falling rapidly as I debate my next move.

When my phone continues to ring, Noah not letting up, I slide my finger across the screen. "Hey."

"Brady, where are you?" I sit up a little straighter when I hear the panic in his voice.

I glance around, not really sure where I am. "I'm over in Weston. I think." Christ, I don't even know how I got here.

"You need to get to the hospital. Brighton and I are here with Melanie."

Hospital?

Panic bursts through me. "What the fuck, Noah? Is Melanie, okay? Is the baby..." Did Melanie have a miscarriage, brought on by anxiety—compliments of my cruel words. Or maybe she's at the hospital to...

My heart lurches and as I grip the steering wheel, my life flashes before my eyes, everything that's important and precious to me, suddenly coming into clear view. My blood drains to my toes, my vision narrowing as I try not to panic.

If anything happens to either of them...

"Which hospital?" I ask, and flick on my signal to pull back into traffic.

"Brigham."

"The baby?"

"We're waiting to hear."

I hear beeping sounds in the background, and a fresh wave of fear washes over me. "Noah…"

"Just get here, Brady. She needs you."

With fear gripping me, I toss my phone onto the passenger seat, and I grasp the steering wheel harder, my earlier conversation with Melanie hovering in the shadows of my brain and haunting me. She needs me. I need her. Jesus Christ, the things I said, things I accused her of. What the hell was I thinking? Melanie is not the kind of woman to get pregnant on purpose, and hell, it takes two to make a baby, right?

With my heart pounding so hard, I can barely hear or see anything around me, I jerk my vehicle to the left, pulling into traffic. Unfortunately, with fear practically debilitating me, I don't see the fast moving vehicle in my blind spot, and the next thing I know, it slams into me, hard, crushing my driver's side door. My car lurches forward, my head banging against the steering wheel. I only come to a stop when I hit the lamppost, and I don't give a shit about my car, or the fact that my arm and head hurt. All I can think about is getting to the hospital.

A knock comes on my window, and the world spins around me as I struggle to open my door, only to find it stuck. How the hell can this be happening? I fight to get my seatbelt off and when I do, I move to the passenger seat and tug on the door handle. Sirens sound in the distance, and my throat tightens. I don't have time for any of this. Melanie needs me and I need to be there for her. I can't fail her.

As every worry I've ever had about failing others comes rushing back to the surface, tears prick my eyes. Someone opens the passenger side door and reaches for me.

"Are you okay, man?" He helps me out, and on the sidewalk, I glance up and down the street, the pavement swaying before my eyes as a crowd forms.

"Yeah, I need to go." I begin to pace, a headache brewing as I try to figure out what to do next. "I have to get to the hospital."

"You're hurt?"

I move my arm, which feels bruised but not broken, and I stare at one point on the sidewalk to stop my head from spinning. "I'm not hurt. I need to get to my girlfriend in the city."

The elderly gentleman puts his hand on my shoulder and I lift my head. His eyes narrow. "You can't go anywhere, dude. Police are here now, and they need to question you. You cut that guy off. I saw the whole thing, and from the way you're wobbling, I think you might have a concussion."

"No, I don't and I have to go."

A police car pulls up in front of my car, and two officers get out. Panic overtakes me, and I glance around, my body shaking as I search for a cab, or a bus.

"Are you hurt?" one officer asks me as the other checks the damage on the car.

"No, I need to go. My girlfriend is in the hospital."

"I need to get some information from you and your vehicle isn't fit for the road." His gaze moves over my face, a careful assessment. "Wait, you're Brady Fisher."

I nod, hoping he's a Bucks fan and that will help me get out of here faster.

I scrub my face, my breath coming in shallow gasps. I need to go. Now. "Yeah, that's me."

He checks out my car. "What happened here?"

I once again tell him that my pregnant girlfriend needs me, and that I need to go, but he doesn't seem to be all that concerned about that.

"Okay, let's get some pictures and paperwork done and this car towed. Then I can let you go."

As my panic escalates, I briefly close my eyes and try to calm myself down. "I really need to go."

His voice is much firmer when he says, "This won't take long."

I reach into my pocket, and grab my phone to call Noah, but I can't find it. Where the hell did it go? Did I even tell him I was on my way? Jesus, I don't even think I hung up before I was sideswiped. I look back into my car, and the world spins around me as I search for my phone. I'm failing Melanie. Jesus Christ, I'm failing her, and there's nothing I can do about it.

Maybe I am no good to anyone.

My legs go weak and the officer puts his hand under my arm to steady me. "I think you need to get checked out."

Dread moves through me when I can't focus enough to find my phone. "I will, later. I need to find my phone."

"Tow truck is on the way," the other officer calls out.

The officer nods toward my glovebox. "I'll need your paperwork."

I drop back down into the passenger seat and open the glovebox to hand over my paperwork. For the next fifteen minutes, pictures are taken and paperwork is exchanged, and a tow truck comes to tow my vehicle away.

After the crowd clears and insurance is called, and I'm free to go, I ask a stranger on the sidewalk to call me a cab. Forty-five minutes later after a very slow and agonizing ride to the city, he drops me at the hospital. I pay him, and hurry inside, even though each step is like a jackhammer to my skull. The place is crowded and I make my way to the nursing station, only to find out Melanie has been discharged.

Jesus Christ.

I grip the counter to hang on as the world tilts on its axis. The one time Melanie needed me and I wasn't even there for her. Maybe she and the baby deserve better, someone who will be there for them in their time of need. Christ, no one has ever been there for her, not even when she was a child, and I'm no better than any of them.

Back outside, I hail another cab, and try to calm my chaotic thoughts as he drives me home. When I get there, I hurry inside, and go straight to my wing of the house, hoping to find Melanie there. I shove the door open and search.

"Melanie," I call out, fear gripping my chest, making breathing near impossible. I gulp air, barely able to fill my lungs as I rush through my place only to find it empty. I head back to the door, ready to storm Noah's place when my feet come to a resounding halt.

"Lanie," I breathe out when I find her standing in my doorway. I lower my eyes to her stomach. "The baby..." My voice is as shaky as my body.

She touches her stomach and her eyes are full of worry, and… tears. "The baby is okay. I was spotting, and it scared me, but we're okay."

A loud, hiccupping sob rises in my throat and with my legs no longer able to support me, I sink to the floor, my body giving out on me. "I'm so fucking sorry, Lanie. You deserve so much better from me."

"Hey," she says quietly, coming to sit next to me, her eyes still watery. She takes my hands.

"I'm so fucking sorry for the things I said to you. You were never a bet to me. I think I was in love with you the first time I ever set eyes on you, and I know you didn't get pregnant on purpose. I also know you think I'm an asshole, a joker, a guy who never takes anything seriously—"

"Brady." I go quiet at the seriousness in her tone. But when warm eyes move over my face, I realize she's not mad. "I don't think any of those things."

I stop breathing as I try to make sense of her words. Why wouldn't she believe any of those things after the way I acted?

"You were never a bet," I manage to push out as my breath comes fast.

"I know, and I know underneath this façade you present to the world, you're an amazing man, with an amazing heart."

I gulp, hardly able to believe what I'm hearing. "You're…you don't…hate me?"

She smiles at me. "No, you see I was recently told I needed to take my own advice so that's what I'm doing. I'm thinking with a clear head and a heart full of love." She cups my face.

"I know who you are, Brady. I know I was never a bet to you, and I also know why you reacted the way you did when I told you I was pregnant."

Another wave of fear burns through my blood. I shake my head, hating myself even though there's so much forgiveness in her heart. "I wasn't there for you, or the baby. I'm so fucking sorry. I wanted to be. I just...couldn't be."

She brushes her fingers through my mess of hair, comforting me. Christ, shouldn't I be the one comforting her. She was the one in the hospital, not me. And after the things I said to her...

"What if..." A sob tightens my throat. "What if I...I can't be what you need? What if we have this baby and something happens to me and I can't be there for you."

"Brady, I know this is scary. Hell, I'm scared too, but you've been letting fear keep you from living for a long time now. Not everyone or everything is your responsibility, especially when you were only eight years old."

"I know but...I was in an accident. I couldn't get to the hospital in time." I swallow against a raw throat. "I'm so fucking terrified, Lanie. You're everything I've ever wanted. The baby too. But I'm so fucking terrified of fucking up. What if something happens to me, what if I can't be there for you guys? I wasn't there today. What if it happens again and again? No one has been there for you, and I was no better. I'm so sorry."

"First, let me say, you're the best man I know, and second let me say it's good to let yourself feel these things. It's healthy. As far as not being there for us, sometimes circumstances are out of our control. Life happens. Accidents happen. Accusations happen. Brady, we both reacted horribly. Our past hurts and fears are why we both lashed out. While emotions are good, I don't want to live in the past anymore. I don't want it ruining our future. We need to feel all the feels, deal with them so they don't come back to haunt us, and learn to move forward. Emotions are not weaknesses, Brady."

Our future.

She's saying we have a future...

"I know I have to make some big changes. I know what's important to me, and I want to be there for those who truly love me. I want to be there for you and our baby. I'm sorry... the hospital..."

"The point is..." She pokes my chest. "You wanted to be there for me." She touches her stomach. "And for our baby. That's what counts and it's not your job to always be there for others."

"Others, no, maybe not. But you and the baby. I want to be there."

She smiles at me and the love and emotions in her eyes soothes my soul and makes me just a little bit less afraid. "I want you to be there too and if something does happen to you, I'll deal with that at the time, and if something happens to me, you'll deal with it. People do find a way to go on. Until then, I think we need to live in the present, and love and care for one another the best way we can."

My heart soars. "I love you, Lanie, and want us to be a family. A real family."

She goes quiet for a long time, and fear grips me. Does she not want that, too?

"I love you too, Brady, but you have to be sure that this is what you want. You have to be sure you're not saying that because of the baby. Because you have this huge sense of responsibility in you and feel it's the right thing to do."

"I'm not." I stand and pull her to her feet. "Come with me, and I'll prove it."

EPILOGUE

Melanie

New Year's Eve:

"I want the biggest wine glass you have," Brighton says as she comes into the kitchen. I turn as she plunks herself down at the island, admiring all the trays of food Gina made for the party. She refused to take payment, because apparently that's what friends do.

Honestly, I've been wanting to have a get together with all my friends, but with the guys' schedule, it was near impossible. I only managed to snag everyone for this New Year's Eve celebration.

"Are you breastfeeding?" I ask and pick up the bottle of wine. I rub my tummy. There will be no wine for me.

"Yes, but I pumped a lot and once I'm done tonight, I'll pump and discard." Brighton winks at me. "Don't worry, I'll teach you all these tricks when your little one comes." I pour the wine and a happy little moan rises in her throat as she drinks. "I can't believe you still don't want to know what you're having."

"We know what we're having," Brady says, entering the kitchen. "A baby." He comes behind the counter, puts his arm around me and gives me a big kiss.

Brighton swirls the wine before taking another drink. "Funny, Brady. Actually, you should just give me the bottle."

I laugh and hand it to her. "You're going to regret this tomorrow."

She points the tip of the bottle at me. "It's your fault, because I'm drinking for you too. Taking one for the team. You're welcome."

Brady and I laugh as she walks into the other room. "Having fun?" he asks. "I know you've been wanting to have this housewarming party forever."

"I am having a blast." I go up on my tiptoes and kiss him, my heart full of love and happiness. The last couple of months have been nothing but a whirlwind of events, and even though I was exhausted and needing to run to the bathroom every five minutes because our baby loves to sit on my bladder, I have never been happier.

When Brady told me he could prove that the baby and I were what he wanted, he drove me straight to the gorgeous home I'm standing in, here in Beacon Hill. Apparently, sneaky guy that he is, he was in the process of buying this home for us, long before he knew about the baby.

He wanted to show me that he loved me, instead of telling me, and he certainly did that, and he's been doing it every day since. While this house is massive, much too big for the three of us, Brady assures me he wants to fill it with kids. We're planning a small wedding after the season is over, and when I say small, we'll likely be able to fill a hockey rink. His entire team and their friends and families are all invited, and I invited Gina, Tania and Trevor. We've all grown close over the last couple of months as well.

He also invited his family from Newfoundland, and it saddens me that none of them had even replied. I never wanted his family out of his life, I just wanted him to set boundaries, because they were taking horrible advantage of him, and he was too afraid to live life because of his responsibilities. He does still send his mother some money to help with repairs and things like that. It's ingrained in him, and he loves her despite everything. He's a good man, and he said it's what his father would have wanted. His uncle, aunts and cousins have all been cut off, and wouldn't you know it, they all found work at the plant. Like I once told him, people do find a way to go on.

"Shall we get in there?" Brady asks. "We have housewarming gifts to open."

"I told them not to bring gifts," I huff out.

He laughs and whacks my ass. "Yeah, but you're kind of glad they did, aren't you?"

I poke him. "Get out of my head, Brady."

"Fine, I'll stay out of your head if you let me in here later." He slides a hand between my legs, and lightly rubs me, which is pretty much all it takes to turn me on. All these hormones have turned me into a crazy nympho, and not only does Brady know it, he likes it. He told me a long time ago after he screeched me in that I was now his nympho. I had no idea that was going to come true.

"I'll have to think about it." He laughs, because I really am a sure thing. "Help me with these."

Dani comes into the kitchen and smiles when she sees us. She truly felt horrible for having to tell me about the bet. After all was said and done, I assured her she did the right thing and we also talked to his friends. They assured us they were just joking around and knew what was happening between us was serious. Heck, I bought them all a beer because Brady did get me to fall in love with him and that was the best thing that ever happened to me.

"Can I help with these?" Dani asks and there's a look of longing on her face as she glances at my growing belly. Did she and her husband plan a family before he died? I'm not sure, but if that's the case, I feel really bad for her. Hopefully someday she'll find love again, and can have the baby she so clearly wants.

"Grab the rolls," I tell her.

Brady reaches for the tray of cheese. "No soft cheese for you, Lanie." I smile, loving the way he takes care of me. I lift my chin to see his face, and the love and emotions in his eyes curl around my heart and squeeze tight.

"I guess you'll have to eat all the cheese, and take one for the team, like Brighton is doing for me."

"You know I'm a team player."

He is a team player, and he's gotten so much better at handling the losses and not thinking the entire responsibility is on his shoulders. He's a better player because of it and the bond with his teammates is even stronger now that he let's them in.

We carry the plates into the other room and set them down. The Christmas tree is still set up and all our housewarming presents are underneath it.

"Open mine first," Conner calls out, and I eye him.

Brady groans as Conner grins like the village idiot. "What did you do?"

"Here, this one." He reaches under the tree and pulls out a big box. He hands it to Brady.

"What is in here and why is it so heavy?"

"You'll have to open it to see."

I laugh because he looks like a kid on Christmas morning. I eye Dani, who whistles innocently. "Oh, you're in on this too?"

"Maybe."

Everyone makes room on the sofa, and Brady and I drop down. "Nothing better jump out at me, Conner," I warn.

"Just open it."

I tear into the paper, and Brady takes the lid off the box. We both glance in, and start laughing.

"Conner, what did you do?" Lanie asks.

Everyone leans toward us, trying to see what's in the box, when Brady pulls out a big codfish, mounted on a board with a plaque beneath. "I love it," Brady laughs.

"Is this the cod...from the night of my celebration?" I ask as I examine the gorgeous taxidermy work. It really is quite spectacular.

Conner looks so proud of himself. "The one and only. Read what it says."

I lean in and read the plaque. "She kissed the cod." I note the date below it. I burst out laughing. "Conner, I absolutely love it. I can't believe you did this."

"To my Newfoundland friends," he toasts and holds up his beer. Everyone salutes to that, and I take a drink of my cranberry juice.

Brady lightly nudges me. "That's the night I told you I loved you."

"Which makes this even more special."

"Are you going to kiss the cod?" Gunther asks.

I wink at Brady. "Yes. I definitely plan to kiss the cod." He grins because he knows exactly what I'm talking about. Brady puts his hand around my neck and pulls me to him, and my heart is so full I'm sure it's going to burst from my chest.

"Kiss the cod. Kiss the cod," Gunther begins to chant, but then stops abruptly. "Wait, are you talking about..."

The room breaks with laughter, and Gunther groans as I press my lips to the man I love, his eyes brimming with a bevy of unchecked emotions as we fall just a little more in love...

***

Thank you so much for reading, **STICKING AROUND, book two in my Boston Bucks series.** I hope you loved this story as much as I loved writing it. Be sure to check out, Sticking Out and Hook 'em Hard (Bang Brother Books), and Stick . The next books in the series, with more to come!

Interested in leaving a review? Please do! Reviews help readers connect with books that work for them. I appreciate all reviews, whether positive or negative.

Happy Reading,

Cathryn

ALSO BY CATHRYN FOX

Boston Bucks

Stick Move

Sticking Around

Sticking Out

Hook 'em Hard

Scotia Storms

Away Game (Rebels)

Warm Up (Rebels)

Crash Course (Rebels)

Home Advantage (Rebels)

Shut Out (Rebels)

Moving Target (Rivals)

Face Off (Rivals)

Scoring Fast (Rivals)

Opposing Teams (Rivals)

Fake Out (Rivals)

Deal Breaker (Rebels)

Hard Burn (Rivals)

End Zone

Fair Play

Enemy Down

Keeping Score

Trading Up

All In

Blue Bay Crew
Demolished
Leveled
Hammered

Single Dad
Single Dad Next Door
Single Dad on Tap
Single Dad Burning Up

Players on Ice
The Playmaker
The Stick Handler
The Body Checker
The Hard Hitter
The Risk Taker
The Wing Man
The Puck Charmer
The Troublemaker
The Rule Breaker
The Rookie
The Sweet Talker
The Heart Breaker

In the Line of Duty
His Obsession Next Door
His Strings to Pull
His Trouble in Talulah

His Taste of Temptation

His Moment to Steal

His Best Friend's Girl

His Reason to Stay

Confessions

Confessions of a Bad Boy Professor

Confessions of a Bad Boy Officer

Confessions of a Bad Boy Fighter

Confessions of a Bad Boy Doctor

Confessions of a Bad Boy Gamer

Confessions of a Bad Boy Millionaire

Confessions of a Bad Boy Santa

Confessions of a Bad Boy CEO

Hands On

Hands On

Body Contact

Full Exposure

Dossier

Private Reserve

House Rules

Under Pressure

Big Catch

Brazilian Fantasy

Improper Proposal

Boys of Beachville

Good at Being Bad

Igniting the Bad Boy

Bad Girl Therapy

Stone Cliff Series:

Crashing Down

Wasted Summer

Love Lessons

Wrapped Up

Eternal Pleasure Series

Instinctive

Impulsive

Indulgent

Sun Stroked Series

Seaside Seduction

Deep Desire

Private Pleasure

Captured and Claimed Series:

Yours to Take

Yours to Teach

Yours to Keep

Firefighter Heat Series

Fever

Siren

Flash Fire

Playing For Keeps Series

Slow Ride

Wild Ride

Sweet Ride

Breaking the Rules:

Hold Me Down Hard

Pin Me Up Proper

Tie Me Down Tight

Stand Alone Title:

Hands on with the CEO

Torn Between Two Brothers

Holiday Spirit

Unleashed

Knocking on Demon's Door

Web of Desire

ABOUT CATHRYN

New York Times and *USA today* Bestselling author, Cathryn is a wife, mom, sister, daughter, and friend. She loves dogs, sunny weather, anything chocolate (she never says no to a brownie) pizza and red wine. She has two teenagers who keep her busy with their never ending activities, and a husband who is convinced he can turn her into a mixed martial arts fan. Cathryn can never find balance in her life, is always trying to find time to go to the gym, can never keep up with emails, Facebook or Twitter and tries to write page-turning books that her readers will love.

Connect with Cathryn:
Newsletter https://app.mailerlite.com/webforms/landing/c1f8n1
Twitter: https://twitter.com/writercatfox
Facebook: https://www.facebook.com/AuthorCathrynFox?ref=hl
Blog: http://cathrynfox.com/blog/
Goodreads: https://www.goodreads.com/author/show/91799.Cathryn_Fox

Pinterest http://www.pinterest.com/catkalen/

Pinterest http://www.pinterest.com/catkalen/

www.ingramcontent.com/pod-product-compliance
Lightning Source LLC
Chambersburg PA
CBHW032238310726
48973CB00008B/2193